It is said that the Devil is in the detail, but what if the Devil was in you?

The world is at war, a war determined to involve Eli, whether he likes it or not. Hitler, his dark army of feral vampires, and even the Devil himself, all conspire against Eli, leaving him no choice but to fight back, risking Malachi's soul in the process.

Eli is determined to find Ethan's father, no matter the cost to himself or Malachi, and in a place filled with death and unending cruelty, Eli realises that some truths should remain buried, and some truths are just too terrible to bear. When the old enemy, demons from Eli's dark past, find him once more, they reveal a secret so impossible, so terrible, that it pushes Eli to the very edge of his endurance. They took his boyfriend from him once, and the secrets that they reveal about the man he once loved threaten to strip Eli of everything that he holds dear, pushing him to the edge of his sanity.

Eli thought that he had nothing left to lose, but at Welwelsburg Concentration Camp, he realises that he was very wrong.

Dead Camp Two
Copyright © 2016 Sean Kerr

ISBN: 978-1-5207-0085-4
Cover art by Latrisha Waters

Published by eXtasy Books Inc or
Devine Destinies, an imprint of eXtasy Books Inc
Look for us online at:
www.eXtasybooks.com or www.devinedestinies.com

Dead Camp Book Two

By

Sean Kerr

Dedication

To my friends Krys and Jayne who read Dead Camp and encouraged me to carry on and tell my story. Thank you for believing in my book and for giving me the inspiration and encouragement to see it through.

To my husband Derek, for his patience while I had this torrid affair with my laptop.

To Craig, well, just for being my friend, and for being well... Craig.

To my Mother and Father for their constant love and support.

But most of all to Laura, no longer with us but always in my heart. She loved Vampires too.

Chapter Sixteen: Dead Camp One

As related by Eli

Welwelsburg Concentration Camp turned my stomach. As I looked down at the sprawling site from our high vantage point atop a hill, I realised how inadequate my plan seemed, though I could not admit that to Malachi. He stood next to me wearing his new body, looking down at the scene before us with equally alarmed eyes.

"The human needs to breathe," I advised.

Mal took a sharp intake of breath. "Fucking hell." It was strange to hear him swear, but I knew it to be a side effect of the possession. All his inhibitions set free.

"Quite. Big. Isn't it."

"Fucking hell."

It had not taken Mal long to adjust to his new body, having already been in and out of it on a number of occasions. The difficulty was trying to get him to behave. Then, once we had persuaded him that having a wank in public was not entirely appropriate, we had to make him man-up. Now that *was* difficult. The epitome of camp, the sight of the outwardly butch looking German soldier strutting his stuff up and down the stairs like some catwalk pansy had me crawling on the floor in a fit of uncontrollable laughter. It took some time, but we got there in the end. Ethan had the bright idea that if Mal screwed up his toes inside his heavy boots, the awkwardness of it, not to mention the pain, would hamper his tendencies to mince. It worked, to a degree, but we did not have the time to perfect his mannerisms. The limp wrists were there to stay.

To compound our expanding list of problems, we also had to deal with the soldier missing from his post for so many days. How could he walk back into the camp without raising suspicions?

Mal searched through the soldier's mind looking for anything we could use, but all he could see was the soldier running through the forest in pursuit of the refugees. Mal could feel his hunger, the excitement of the chase, the thrill of torture. That gave me an idea. I did not like it and I felt sure Mal would like it even less, so I laid out my thoughts before him and hoped he and Ethan would understand my reasoning.

My idea was simple. The soldier had been in the thick of it, pursuing his prey through the forest. So what if a group of refugees accosted the soldier and left him for dead deep in the forest? We had to create a story, one where the soldier split from the main group, where the refugees beat him into unconsciousness and left him for dead in a secluded ditch. He could have been lying there, bleeding and comatose in that impenetrable darkness for days without anyone finding him. Disorientated and weak, it would have taken him days to find his way back to the camp.

Okay. So believable story, but the soldier looked unmarked and unharmed, the perfect specimen of Arian perfection. Then I let rip with the rest of my plan.

Ethan got it straight away, even before I got to the more difficult bits. His face darkened and I could see the idea troubled him deeply, his humanity leeching out toward me with an accusing finger.

"It's all I've got," I said pathetically, not particularly happy myself.

"He's a human being." Ethan's compassion, especially for

a German, the German who helped to hunt and kill such innocents, astonished me. It made me feel even more like a monster.

"He killed them, slaughtered children, do you think he stopped to consider his actions for one moment? Do you think he regrets killing those children? He is a Nazi, he is a real monster, do not feel compassion for a creature such as him, save it for those who deserve it." Scathing words that I should have tempered, but I felt shitty enough without his disapproval.

"Even monsters deserve compassion." Ethan's words cut through me like a wooden stake. His eyes bore into me, unwavering. They demanded I find another way, and of course, he was right.

I tore myself away from his penetrating eyes and clamped my hands to my head as though I could squeeze out the answer.

Squeeze out the human.

"Mal, come out of there for a moment." The soldier blurred and Mal extricated himself with a loud pop. He was getting better at it. Before the soldier had time to recover, I grabbed him by the shoulders, my vampire there in all its full glory ,and his eyes widened in terror at the sight of my black eyes and sharp teeth.

"What are you doing?" Mal squealed, all girl and no man.

I looked into the soldier's terrified eyes and felt my thoughts enter him. He struggled against my intrusion but his poor human soul was no match for my hypnotic power. I was Menarche. I was irresistible to all humans, and boy was I irresistible to men.

"You will feel no pain," I intoned softly as the dreaminess of my voice began to crush his consciousness.

"Pain?" Mal gasped but I paid him no heed, my concentration totally focussed on the German.

3

"When you awake you will feel no pain, you will feel nothing."

"I will... feel... nothing," intoned the soldier from deep within his fugue like state.

"Your mind will sleep, let the blackness wash over you, let your mind crawl away into the void until I call for you, until then you do not exist, you have no body, you are nothing. My mind is in your mind. Let me feel your pain, let me shelter you from harm." I let him go and he just sat there staring into space, his mind closed down, his senses asleep, nothing but an empty mindless shell.

"Clever," smirked Ethan. "You're not just a pretty face are you?"

My mouth twitched into the semblance of a reassuring smile. Ethan could see I was trying to make things as easy for the human as I could, and while I appreciated his words, it didn't detract from the horror I was about to commit.

I picked up the soldier and threw him against the wall using but a fraction of my vampire strength. He hit the wall with a sickening crunch.

"What are you doing?" Mal darted between us, imploring me to stop.

"He has to look the part, Mal." Ethan tried to sound reassuring, but he failed to convince.

"Get out of my way, Mal—it has to be this way. Move!"

The soldier's eyes stared wide and unseeing, oblivious to the pain that pulsed down his back as his body slammed against the wall, pain that I felt for him. The revulsion of my actions stung my eyes as I approached him and lashed out with a vicious kick to his ribs that cracked loudly before my merciless boot.

The pain surged through my chest. Blackness blurred the corners of my eyes as ripples of agony stabbed my brain.

Another kick to the face, blood sprayed across the wall

and floor. My vampire stirred, roused by the scent of spilled life, my nostrils flaring as the bitter coppery stench hit the back of my throat. I tried to calm my vampire, forced it to lie dormant as my fists pummelled the soldiers face, repeatedly, red matter staining my knuckles. Eyes looked at me, wide and uncomprehending, eyes that felt no pain, eyes as dead as the heart within my chest.

Every blow that met his frail human skin ate away at my coveted humanity. I felt every blow, experienced his agony, my mind sheltering his from the torture I inflicted, taking the pain into myself.

I was hitting myself, all my anger, all my hatred, all my self-loathing, my loneliness, encapsulated in each blow. Excruciating pain, the pain of a human, I was human, feeling for a human. It was no more than I had wanted.

I did terrible things, Ethan. Slap! I just wanted to be touched, Ethan. Crunch! I wanted to be needed, Ethan. Squelch!

His lower lip split beneath my fingers and my hands trembled as the soldier slid onto his side, blood pumping wasted onto the floor. Another kick to his face shattered his nose. Dark ugly bruises already formed on his face, his left eye nothing but a bag of weeping flesh, swollen and pulsing with blood.

And still I went on.

Gideon left me, Ethan. Snap!

I kicked his arms, his legs and my voice filled Alte as I screamed my defiance, screamed my anger and fury. Such cruelty. Such terrible cruelty.

I found myself on my knees holding my weeping face in bloodied hands, my sobs convulsing through my body. The arms that found my shoulders to embrace me belonged to Ethan.

"It's over, Eli, it's over."

His gentle words penetrated my skull and I heard them, I just didn't believe them. It was not over. It would never be over, not as long as those Menarche bastards walked the earth, not as long as Hitler cut across the planet like a scythe. It would never be over.

It would never be over as long as I remained unloved.

It took me some time to gather myself, and when I did, I sat quietly in a corner as Mal re-entered the shattered body of the soldier. I could not speak. I could not look at Ethan. I did not want the pain to end.

Eli must suffer. Suffer little children. I was a child.

The German could still walk and talk, but he looked a mess. Mal said the soldier felt nothing, that his mind was far away dreaming, but it did not console me. The memory of that act would haunt my every waking moment, forever.

And so we flew to Welwelsburg, the Mal soldier clasped around my neck, the wind freeze-drying the blood that oozed from a plethora of wounds on his face. I found a vantage point, high above the valley where Welwelsburg Castle and its death camp lay beneath us, and we stood looking down on the place in silence.

It was huge. The castle itself was set above the camp on a small hill surrounded by a thick band of pine trees. The monolith, in the shape of an imposing triangular structure, dominated the skyline, its dark foreboding turrets reaching its black fingers into the night sky. Lights burned fiercely like eyes in all three turrets, glaring down on the human tragedy at its feet, ever watchful of that which lay in its long shadow.

The camp lay sprawled at the base of the hill, surrounded by enough barbed wire to shred the planet. Four wooden watchtowers stood guard, one at each corner, their powerful arc lights constantly scanning the surrounding countryside like great white tongues of impending death, ready to vaporise anything they touched.

A group of a dozen grey, windowless boxes lay in neat long rows to the east and to the west. I discerned another batch of larger buildings and outhouses, the same drab on drab colour. Windows blazed brightly in one large square building around which huddled a group of ambulances. I supposed even Nazis fell ill.

A large enclosure in the northeast quadrant, itself fenced off with a high ring of barbed wire, contained hundreds of black mounds, unidentifiable even to my fantastic eyes. There was something deeply unsettling about that area, the abandonment of it — looking at it made me feel so empty.

A thick cloying odour drew my gaze toward a building tucked away to the northwest area and my skin prickled with irrational fear. It was rectangular with a pitched red tiled roof. A tall chimney protruded from the far end that spewed forth a thick grey smoke, the plume draping itself over the camp like some huge portentous umbrella, spreading its insidious tendrils coiling across the landscape. The smell made my vampire shiver uncontrollably. It smelled of burning and death.

A railway track wound its way through the valley, ending at the south gate by a ramp. A huge round turntable with a double line of tracks terminated the line. Soldiers milled about behind the huge fortified gates, flapping their arms against the freezing wind that bit at their frail human bodies, and it seemed to me they were waiting for something. Suddenly, in the distance, the whistle of a train pierced the cold night, and immediately the soldiers sprang into action, unlocking the metal gates and heaving them open. A spiral of steam belched through the trees, cutting a path through the forest toward the camp, and I realised our chance was at hand, the arrival of the train the perfect distraction for our infiltration.

"Mal, get down there now while they are busy."

Mal looked at me from within his swollen face, and despite the bloated mess, I could still see the look of worry and concern radiating from his human eyes.

"I know," I said kindly, "you be careful, too. Find me as soon as you learn anything." I leaned over and kissed him gently on the cheek and he touched the spot with a trembling hand.

"I do love you, you know." He used simple words to frame a complex statement and my stomach churned.

"I know." What was I doing sending him into that place, into a world full of demons, full of evil so dark it could destroy us both at a whim? Yet I still could not bring myself to say those words back to him. I loved Mal, yes, but not that way. I watched him descend the hill without a word and every now and again, he would glance back with that adoring look that filled me with so much guilt. There was nothing left to say, nothing that would mean anything. Nothing that would help. Mal was on his own and I prayed to a God that never listened to keep him safe and bring him home. Mal and I needed to have a conversation, one I was dreading and it would hurt him more than any Menarche or demon. As he disappeared into the darkness, I realised that even if he did come home safely, I would probably lose him forever anyway.

As I crept down the hill toward the camp, I could not take my eyes off its sprawling, suffocating evil, leaching the land of life and hope. I knew the place existed, I knew the Nazis had claimed the area as their own, but I had chosen to ignore it. I chose to stay away, to overlook the devil in my own back yard.

Daniyyel was correct. My apathy was shameful. From time to time, I had hunted around the area, fed off soldiers, hypnotised them into fucking me in the woods, but always ignoring the bigger picture. I had blocked it from my consciousness — it did not matter to me. Therefore, it was not important to me. Welwelsburg was nothing more than a larder, a fast food outlet and as I watched the train grinding to a noisy stop I truly realised what I was doing. It was as if a veil of shit peeled away from my eyes and I could truly see for the first time, and it terrified me. Years of shelter, of safety, of solitude, of hiding, were all about to end. My existence as I knew it was over. And it was time to pay the ferryman.

The lumbering locomotive with its four long cargo carriages screamed through the night, grinding to a noisy, clanking standstill, and a group of soldiers moved in quickly to unhook the locomotive. Slowly the engine chugged onto the circular dais and I watched fascinated as the engine began to turn slowly with squeals of metallic protest that sounded like some ancient dinosaur awaking form its slumber. As the platform turned, the engine began to align with a second set of tracks that ran parallel to the first, and with a loud juddering bang the tracks connected and the engine began its journey back the way it came. The technology of man never failed to amaze me.

The doors of the cargo containers slid open with a loud grinding screech that set my teeth on edge. The smell hit me instantly, the stale sour stench of death and rotting meat, human meat. I crouched low, unseen, hunkered down behind a container listening to the soldiers barking their harsh, brutal orders into the containers. Then I saw them, feet stepping down from the containers, so many bare feet belonging to crowds of never-ending people. Those poor unfortunate souls, crammed into each container like so much meat hanging in a butcher's. It was all I could do to stop myself from ripping the carriages and the soldiers apart with my bare hands. They were people, living breathing people, treated worse than animals.

The smell of death mingled headily with the smell of piss and shit. The air buzzed with the stench. With so many people jammed into one small space, it was a wonder that any of them survived at all. As I prepared to move out from under the carriage, I saw a body collapse to the floor, a woman, wrapped in a thin shawl, her face a twisted torment of utter terror and defeat. Her gaze found mine. There was nothing left but despair in those eyes, a hopelessness that seeped into my soul and tore at my heart. Many hands reached down to help, but a soldier screamed for them to leave her where she fell. I saw a pair of black boots approach the woman's head, then I saw the muzzle of a riffle.

"Get up." Already the light was fading from her eyes and I knew she was dying. A black boot kicked her in the chest and she flopped onto her back, raising a pathetically weak hand toward her tormentor. There was so much desperation in that gesture, so much pleading in a prayer for mercy that went unheeded. The muzzle blazed, I saw the fire erupt from its tip before I heard the explosion and I saw her head burst before the ringing had stopped in my ears. Her body lay broken and the boots walked casually away from the bloody scene. Pain stabbed through the palms of my hands as my nails flashed sharp with anger, digging into my flesh.

With a tremendous effort, I swallowed my rage, forced the vampire that seethed within to calm and concentrated for all I was worth on the task before me. The smell of blood, the rank odour of death, the cruelty, all conspired to blow my cover even before I started. My monster diminished and the flesh on my hands healed instantly. I blocked the smell from my senses. I denied my nose the tang of blood and I denied myself the satisfaction of ripping that murdering cunt limb from limb. I wanted to rip off his head and piss in the stump. I wanted to tear his still beating heart out from his spineless body and shove it up his tight asshole. I wanted... I wanted...

I wanted to get into the camp. I needed to blend into the throng of desperate humans, become one of the desperate.

I could do desperate.

Silently, I crawled up the side of the carriage and crept onto the roof, slithering through an open vent to drop down into suffocating darkness.

Nothing living remained inside. Even with the large square of the door open to the world outside, the light seemed afraid to penetrate the dank interior. The sight of so many wasted lives scattered across the rough floor made me feel deeply ashamed, and no matter how hard I tried, I could not keep the rot of human fluids from infiltrating my nasal passages. Flies darted around the carcasses, their incessant buzzing amplified in the confined space. It was a slaughterhouse.

The body of an old man lay next to my feet. His skin fell loose from his face in heavy wrinkled folds, his body deflated like a discarded balloon. He had once been a large man but malnutrition had whittled him down to nothing but bones and desiccated organs held together by a loose bag of skin.

"Forgive me, sir." I bent down and took off his filthy coat. There was a crude handwritten name badge on the front of the garment together with a yellow Star of David sewn to the lapel. The dead man's name was David Minkes. I repeated his name in my head repeatedly and as I pulled the coat over my own, I swore to his dead soul I would never forget his name. I scooped up handfuls of filth from the floor, slathering human excrement mixed and mud over my face and through my hair, making sure that my own pale skin, hands and face lay hidden beneath layers of filth. I did the same for my clothes and my shoes until I looked just like the prisoners, a shadow remnant of the human race.

In a blur of super human speed, I left the carriage and entered humanity. No one showed me the slightest bit of notice. Essentially, I was just another prisoner, another down-trodden human joining the rout of mankind.

I stood amid a crowd of grey, dirty, hungry creatures that once resembled people. We stood on the ramp in silent expectation, fear riding the crowd in palpable waves of nauseating dread. Children whimpered, but the adults could do nothing to allay their terror. A heavy fat man of an officer, wearing an immaculate SS uniform, waddled to the front of the ramp and held up a cane above our heads, and a terrified hush crushed all under his shadow. I could smell his sweat and something else, excitement, sexual excitement, and I could see the bulge that grew at the front of his trousers. He was getting off on the terror he instilled—it thrilled him. I could smell it on him.

Fat greasy fuck. His nose was so fat it looked like a bell-end. If I got the chance, I would kill the fat bastard. He wiped his sweaty face with a dirty handkerchief. Much to my disgust, he sniffed it.

"I am your Blockfürher." Faces remained as passive and unimpressed as possible. The crowd just looked at him through dead uncaring eyes, but their faces resisted the overwhelming urge to show fear. Their blatant defiance made the fat man sneer angrily and right then at that moment, I felt an overwhelming sense of pride for those poor tormented people, standing there so proud against the tyrant. It was but a small gesture, one that the grotesque blob felt. Just behind him was a man, thin and gaunt but wearing a black and white stripped gown. A prisoner of some sort—I had no idea why he would be standing amid the Nazis. When he saw the silent look from the prisoners and the fat bastard's irritation at the crowd's lack of humility, he could not help but smirk, lowering his head into his chest to hide his amusement.

"What I say here is law," continued the greasy twat. "You do not sleep unless I say so, you do not eat unless I say so, you do not shit unless I say so and you do not piss unless I say so. However, you may die any time you wish. You, come forward."

He pointed to a young man in his late teens, his attire hanging loosely from his bony frame. He staggered forward with a severe limp and I noticed his right foot twisted cruelly. The Blockfürher pulled a small silver revolver from around his copious waist and brought it to bare against the young lads head.

Bang!

The bullet went through his forehead, exploding out of the back to shower those around him with blood and bits of brain. A scream of shock exploded from the crowd, the sound rippling outward. That made the fat bastard smile with approval.

He was going to die by my hand and it would not be pleasant.

"Welwelsburg is a work camp, and trust me when I say that you *will* be put to work. We have no room here for those incapable of satisfying our labour needs." He shook the revolver in front of his face before putting it back in its holder. He indicated for the black and white dressed man to move forward.

"Shortly you will be split into groups, and this man will divide you between the various barracks that the German Empire has so generously provided for you. He is the head Kapo. Each barrack will have a Kapo, but all report back to this... gentleman." He slapped his cane into the prisoner's chest, making him flinch. "And he in turn reports back to me. Once split into groups, stripped, shaved, and disinfected, your Kapo will direct you to your barrack where you may sleep. Make the most of it, you will need it." The fat bastard finished with a last derisive sneer, his piggy eyes devouring his captives hungrily, then with an abrupt turn on his heels, he marched away.

Oozed away.

Slithered away.

Fat fucking cunt.

The relief emanating from the crowd at his departure washed over me, but it was short lived as a much younger soldier came forward holding a short black stick. It looked like a magic wand.

Houdini started to call us forward one by one, indicating which way we should go with a flick of his wand, left or right toward the relevant Kapo. This interminable process seemed to drag on for hours and I could not decipher the process behind the selection at first, until I noticed the colour of the triangles on the chest of each prisoner.

Most prisoners wore the yellow Star of David, a Hebrew symbol identifying the wearer as a Jew. Occasionally a prisoner wearing a black triangle moved to the front, corralled into a dark corner where he cowered in the darkness overlooked by two armed guards. Green badges joined the head Kapo. Men wearing pink triangles suffered the same fate as those wearing black, huddled together in a corner at gunpoint. But the Nazis hit and slapped them repeatedly, enjoying their cruel sport, laughing as the pitiful men cowered from their fists.

Those men with the pink triangles, they were like *me*. Call it instinct, call it gay radar but I knew, without doubt, they were like me. I could see it in their eyes. I could read it in their mannerisms. I felt it in my heart. They were gay. Pink triangles meant homosexual. I watched their terror, their bodies trembling with fear. I felt their hopelessness and their despair and I wanted to weep for them.

When my turn came, they took me to the right to join a group of some thirty inmates. They arranged us in three rows of ten, then the Kapo came forward, up and down each line making notes of our names. With the roll call finished, the Kapo ordered us to follow him in single file. As we moved away, I could not help but look back at the group with the pink triangles cowering in the dark. I felt for them, I felt for them all, but I was afraid of what would happen to those men in particular. Two of them stood erect suddenly, a look on their faces that said *no more,* and I shivered. I had spent many lifetimes with others judging me for what I was, and those sentiments rang fresh and true in my head every single day. The couple, in their mid-sixties, reached out a hand to each other and stood there proud and defiant, holding each other, loving each other. My heart swelled with something that hurt intensely. I wanted to smile at them, to show them I understood — that I understood their love. They looked at me and smiled with such warmth, with such recognition, and the emotion of that look began to engulf me, tear at my heart with fingers of pain. A soldier marched forward and hit them both with the butt of his riffle until they slumped to the floor, but neither man uttered a sound, not a gasp, or a whimper.

I had to look away before my eyes gave away my anger. I had to look away before I lost myself in the red of blood.

We came to the area I had seen from the hill, the lonely area enclosed by barbed wire, and the Kapo produced a heavy bunch of keys and opened the gate.

"Inside!" One by one, we entered the enclosure. It was so dark, but I could see everything. Those black indistinguishable mounds viewed from a distance suddenly took form with sharp horrific clarity, and there were hundreds of them. Everywhere there were great mounds of discarded clothes.

"Take off your clothes and leave them in one pile, then stand by the fence." When we didn't move fast enough, the Kapo lashed out at the nearest inmate with a thick wooden baton, sending him gasping to the ground in agony. Everyone began to strip down quickly after that. It was freezing cold and I feared that some would not survive the night. My body stood out white in the darkness but then so did the others, their bodies hanging in loose bags of skin and bone with barely enough strength left in them to keep them upright. They all looked as dead as me. We were dead men walking.

Groups of men huddled together for warmth, shambling through the bitter cold as the Kapo marched us to another building. A line of ten prisoners, all dressed in the same black and white stripped overalls as the Kapo, stood to attention, each holding a pair of silver sheers, the metal glinting maliciously in the moonlight.

"Time for a haircut, courtesy of our Blockfürher. Form an orderly queue and move forward when indicated. Kneel with your back toward your barber. Do not speak—do not make a sound. You are nothing but sheep and I am your shepherd. Once shorn, move into the showers behind you. At the other end, we will issue your new clothes. Now move!"

That a fellow prisoner, another human, should show so much contempt toward its own kind, disgusted me. War always brought out the worst in man, but that bastard was enjoying himself too much. He also had a green triangle sewn to the front of his black and white uniform. Yellow Star of David for Jews, pink triangles for homosexuals, so what manner of human being did the green triangles represent? Twat?

Ten at a time moved forward to kneel before the other

prisoners. Frightened, trembling hands used primitive clippers to shear the hair from our scalps and the reluctant barbers tried so hard to be gentle, but it did not prevent bloody cuts or flaps of torn raw skin catching in the blunt, rusty instruments.

I was in trouble. Even before my first night was over, I faced my first real crisis. When injured, my flesh regenerated very, very quickly.

I knelt on the hard gravel, hands clasped between my knees. I felt the cold metal pressed against my head and heard the clicking sound of it eating. Wisps of thick hair tumbled before my eyes. Unskilled hands hacked away at my beautiful locks and I felt guilty thinking it would grow back thick and lustrous soon enough. Even with the threat of discovery so close, my vanity could not help but define me. Suddenly I felt the blades dig into my skin and a thick rivulet of blood, black against my white skin, trickled down my neck.

I could also feel the cut instantly knitting back together.

"Aluka," the young man whispered as his hands faltered. I closed my eyes, waiting for the inevitable scream, furious with myself for failing so quickly, but it never came. Gentle fingers brushed my scalp and the sound of a thundering heart beating against a hollow chest almost deafened my ears. He was holding his breath. I moved away quickly, daring a sideways glance at the stranger as I ducked into the showers. He was such a young thing, frail and delicate, beautiful. He would have been lovely in another life. To my surprise, I read no fear in his face, just a burning curiosity behind his eyes and an intelligence that saw me for what I was. As I slipped into the showers, he offered me a gentle, kind smile, and the corners of my mouth flickered upward in response. I was grateful for his discretion and hoped I would have the opportunity to thank him, but in a place already full of horrors, I was the least of his troubles.

I walked into a tunnel lined with cold white tiles. Showerheads protruded intermittently from the walls and they sprayed forth a noxious liquid that stank, a mix of disinfectant and ammonia. Prisoners standing along the opposite wall, each wielding long handled brooms, pushed us under the showerheads with brutal force, scrubbing our bodies with the rough unforgiving bristles. My hard vampire flesh thought nothing of the assault but I made a show of discomfort and pain all the same, unlike the others who suffered the burning purification in its entire skin-blistering entirety.

Many Nazi twats were going to die by my hand.

Once we were pushed unceremoniously from the showers, the icy winter night bit into our bones with hungry teeth. Steam roiled from bare flesh as March reasserted its dominance over mankind in a cruel reminder of nature's harsh majesty. We queued at a trestle table where more prisoners thrust black and white striped uniforms into our eager hands before the Kapo ushered us back into regimented lines to dress. The thin rough cloth offered us little protection against the bitter chill, but it was better than a poke in the eye with a sharp stick.

The Kapo led us toward one of the numerous windowless structures situated in the east quadrant. From my vantage point in the hills, I had thought those buildings to be storage facilities, and as it turned out, I was right. They were storage facilities for humans.

Bare electric bulbs enclosed by wire cages illuminated our dire surroundings. Rows of wooden shelves, stacked one on top of the other, filled the interior in three rows. Each shelf had a thick layer of straw with rough blankets strewn across them to create crude mattresses. Pale, desperate faces peered out from many of the shelves, cattle herded into one cramped space like so many factory hens, and yet again, I tasted the foul disappointment of man's compassion grate against my teeth.

"You will find a bed where you can and you will sleep. Sleep now and sleep well, for tomorrow there is much work required of you and you *will* work hard." The filthy creature lashed out and grabbed a nearby man, an elderly Jew who could barely stand, he was so frail. The Kapo gripped him by the back of the neck and pulled him close so their faces almost touched and the look of terror on the old man's face sickened me.

Spittle sprayed from the Kapo's lips as he growled at the Jew. "You belong to me now, and I will not take idleness kindly." He threw the hapless man roughly to the floor. I went to his side while others scuttled away from him, frightened of the Kapo's wrath. I could not blame them. The old man's hand felt fragile and brittle in my fingers as I helped him to his feet and all the while, the Kapo sneered at me, his cold eyes glinting darkly.

The Kapo stepped toward me, his hand raised. For a moment I contemplated ripping him apart there and then but I had to calm myself, I had to remind myself of my purpose, I had to be satisfied I would rip his arm off and shove it up his ass soon enough. The Kapo grinned, a self-satisfied smirk I wanted to swipe from his face.

"Sleep, all of you, while you still have the option of waking up." As he said those words, his eyes did not leave my face and I was forced to do something I had never done before—I backed down, humbled myself before that thing masquerading as a human, that piece of shit on legs. I bowed my head in supplication, I slumped my shoulders in a show of submissiveness that went against everything I believed in. That nasty squelching sound that assaulted my ears was the sound of me swallowing my pride.

With the show over, my roommates ambled toward the shelves and two, three, four at a time squeezed themselves into the cramped spaces. The Kapo chuckled to himself and left, turning the lights off as he did so. A collective groan sighed through the cramped space as the darkness gave voice to undigested fears and panic. The darkness pulsed with it. My eyes could see perfectly through the gloom and it would have been nothing for me to guide those individuals left struggling in the blackness to the safety of a shelf, but instead, I watched them fall over each other in a desperate attempt to reach safety.

And all the time I kept telling myself I could not give myself away, not yet.

The old man—he was still standing beside me. He looked ill and very weak. I gripped his arm gently and he jumped, startled by my touch.

"It's okay." I pulled him toward an empty shelf just behind me. "That's it, careful now—just a few more steps and you can rest." He could barely put one foot in front of the other. Exhausted, malnourished, beaten and just plain old, the man had no strength left.

Fuck it, I thought. It was dark, who the fuck would see. I lifted him in my arms, carried him to the shelf and laid him atop the straw mattress. He groaned as his old, brittle bones creaked with arthritis, then sighed with relief as his body sank into the soft straw.

"Thank you, thank you for helping me." Even his voice was frail. I crawled onto the shelf beside him and cradled his head in my lap. His flesh felt cold, not a sensation I expected in a human. His deep-set eyes, once so blue and alive in youth, were dull and glazed over with cataracts that made him look like one already dead. Flesh, once tight and vibrant, now fell wrinkled and dry to the touch, almost powdery. Old age remained a cruel, unrelenting bastard.

"Don't mention it... please... I mean it. What's your name?" I found myself stroking his head, fingers caressing the stubble that once held a mop of proud grey hair.

"Jakob, Jakob Eisenhardt."

"I am very pleased to meet you, Jakob Eisenhardt. I am Eli and I want you to close your eyes and sleep."

A feeble hand swatted an invisible fly.

"Sleep is for the fishes, and I fear I will sleep soon enough, so indulge an old man with little time left, and let me talk while my lips can still form words."

I could not help but laugh. I loved the Jews, such a pragmatic race.

"So tell me, Jakob, do you have family?" I felt his body tense beneath me and I immediately regretted my stupid, inane question. "I'm sorry, my friend... it seems the art of polite conversation is something I need to practise, forgive me."

"No, no... not at all, it is a reasonable enough question in unreasonable times. Yes, I have family. We fled to Poland, but my wife was murdered and my son, Max, was captured. They took him to Auschwitz."

"I'm sorry."

"Don't be, it helps an old man to remember such things."

"What happened?" I found I wanted to know his story. It took me by surprise. For so long I had cut myself off from humanity, from the emotion that being with them elicits, and then I found myself bathing in it, swamped by the overbearing weight of their pain in that hellish prison. It surprised me even more that his hand should reach out for my own, that it should hold onto my unyielding flesh with such grim determination.

"We fled from our home—with the passing of the Nuremburg Laws we had no choice but to flee for our freedom, to Poland. Huh! Who knew? The invasion was swift and merciless. Thousands died. My wife, they murdered her before my eyes, they left my son, Max and I for dead, bullet wounds in each of us. The Nazis buried us in a mass grave. We lay there, buried beneath friends, pretending to be dead. Max would whisper in my ear and beg me to be still. The wound in my stomach, the pain was unbearable, but God's will be done, three days later my son pulled me from the grave and patched me up as best he could."

I could feel his heart beating faster beneath my fingers as he recounted his dreadful story. "Your son must be a remarkable boy."

"Yes, yes he is, my son, my Max, he is extraordinary to me..."

A tear trickled down his face and his lips trembled as he tried to speak the words he so desperately wanted to express.

"He pulled me into an abandoned farm house. I could barely walk. I had lost so much blood. He... he wanted to scout the village to find me antibiotics, and I held on to his hand so tight, desperate for him not to leave me. I pleaded with him but my son, my Max—he could not stand to see me in such pain. He left me and I watched from a window as they captured him and loaded him onto a truck. As they pushed him into the back of that vehicle, he looked back, just the once and he winked. It was a small thing but I saw it. I have not seen him since."

"He sounds like a strong man."

His eyes glittered as he looked up into my face and a smile spread across his old features.

"Yes. A man, yes, strong... intelligent. I know, in my heart, that Max will find a way to escape, nothing, nobody will keep him locked up for long, I feel it."

"Hold onto that feeling, my friend. Let it comfort you."

"As I find comfort in you?" His words struck me deep and I found they stung. It had been a very long time since anyone had found solace in my arms, or since I cradled anybody for more than my own sexual motivations. I was beginning to realise my emergence back into the world of the living was going to be a difficult, painful experience.

"What is it with these Kapo guys anyway? They are dressed like prisoners, and yet they treat us no better than the Nazis do. What's that all about?"

"Mankind never fails to shame itself before the eyes of God."

"I'm beginning to see that."

"The Kapos are identified by green triangles. They are convicts, criminals, put into a position of power by their Nazi masters. Who better to police us undesirables than our very own outcasts and misfits, hmm?"

A violent coughing fit suddenly coursed through his frail body and I clung onto him tightly for fear he would fall off the shelf. Cold beads of perspiration exploded across his flesh and I could hear his heart beat stutter within his chest. I cradled a dying man in my arms. The vampire was helpless.

"I'm sorry... I'm so sorry..."

"No, my friend, it is I who should apologise for making you tell me your story. But you must sleep, please, rest, regain your strength."

His body relaxed into me and I could feel sleep beginning to take him.

"I... will not argue with you."

"I have a feeling that is unusual for you."

He chuckled gently. "I wish I had known you in my youth, my friend. I like you."

"In another lifetime, old man, in another life."

The coughing fit returned, fiercer than before and his whole body shook with the pain. Weak hands reached out toward me so I pulled him close into my chest, trying to use my own strength to quell the spasms that wracked through his body. He coughed up blood. I could smell it on me. It smelled thick and glutinous — it reeked of death. I rocked him back and forth, his breathing heavy and laboured between painful bouts of retching, and I would have given anything at that moment to take his suffering away.

The coughing started to lessen and his body began to relax, to become limp, but I could sense his strength leaving, feel his life fleeing his body. I clung to him tighter, thinking that perhaps I could force his life to stay within his damaged frame, willing his life to stop bleeding from his flesh, prevent his existence from pouring away between my fingers. But no matter how hard I tried, I could not stop it. My mouth fell open, a cry of desperation sticking to the back of my throat.

"Max..." Then his body stiffened as a wave of convulsions flowed through him, his bare feet thumping violently against the wood of the shelf.

I tried to hold him. I tried to stop his thrashing, but I could not.

And then he stopped. My friend looked up into my face, his arms limp at his sides and a faint smile crawled across his blood-smeared lips. The last of his air hissed through his blue mouth and his eyes glazed over as the last of his life ebbed away.

I sat in the darkness, holding the body of Jakob Eisenhardt, cursing the world for forcing me back into it.

How I hated the world.

Chapter Seventeen: Dead Camp Two

As related by Malachi

Self-obsessed, arrogant, selfish, vain, all words that adequately described Eli. Even as I walked toward the camp, he stood there watching me, posturing, loving himself. I suppose he thought himself to be the most beautiful thing on that hillside.

And the trouble was, he was right.

Fit. Oh my. I never tired of his bulging muscles. And that meatsicle between his legs was to die for. And how could one ever tire of those eyes?

That brief moment when I made love to him, using that fabulously Germanic body. I had waited so many years for an opportunity like that. Just to be able to touch him and actually feel his flesh, to feel the hardness beneath my hands, to taste his skin against my lips. He felt so good. When I entered him, it felt like nothing I had experienced before. As I pushed deeper it felt I wanted to enter him entirely, that I could not get enough of me inside him and I pushed harder and harder and still it was not enough. I lost myself in him. And for those few precious moments, I was his.

If I said yes to that angel, at least I could do so knowing I had fulfilled my one wish, my one true desire.

But as I looked at him standing there so perfectly, looking at me with his big soulful eyes, my stolen moment of pleasure felt like a hollow victory.

I wanted him to love me so very much, to love me the

same way I loved him. I risked my soul for him to love me. I thought I could make him feel something, I thought that to be human, to make love to him as a human, would be enough. And if I were human, he would have to make me like him, make me a vampire, because he would love me so very much.

I would make myself a monster if it meant him loving me.

In the beginning, he was full of hatred, hatred for the world, hatred for himself and hatred for me. It was as though he could not stand the sight of me. On more than one occasion, he told me to go, screamed at me to leave him and I did try, once.

That little episode did not end so well.

We came to Alte from London, and Eli was a broken man, fragile, a total mess. I knew very little of the cataclysmic events that took place in that far off city, and I only knew snippets of what transpired between Eli and Gideon. As far as Eli was concerned, Gideon had left him, and that was all I needed to know.

I figured Eli would tell me in time, as our friendship grew, as he learned to trust me, that the full story would be forthcoming. But instead, his mood deepened and I watched helpless as he tumbled further into despair. So complete was the blackness that gripped him that he refused to feed. He looked terrible. And in his case that took some doing. Black rings accentuated deep sunken eyes and cheekbones protruded from skin so white and so taut that it seemed always to be on the verge of splitting. His vampire teeth were permanently out then, jutting over dry and cracked lips. Even his gums seemed to be receding. Eli was decaying before my eyes.

"Eli, you look awful, nothing but skin and bone. There will be nothing left of you before long." He looked at me with such eyes, desperately haunted eyes and it frightened me.

"I hope for nothing less."

Oh my. Oh gosh. As if I were not already worried enough.

"You need to feed. You need to make yourself strong again."

The vampire flickered across his face and I realised for the first time just how indistinguishable his two aspects were becoming, as though his pain were manifesting itself as the vampire, permanently.

"I *need* to suffer! I need to become dust! And whether or not I choose to feed has fuck-all to do with you. Don't ever presume to know me or what I need, is that clear?"

I thought I saw a glimmer of regret overshadow the darkness that twisted his face. I thought I saw repentance in his eyes, but he shrank away from me as though afraid. He clutched his hands to his chest, wringing them anxiously, and for a moment, he looked poised to say something, but then he turned and fled up the stairs in a blur of speed. Nothing I could say would penetrate his head, and nothing I could say would make any difference.

I found Alte a lonely place that night. My head felt positively giddy, it spun with so many thoughts. What had happened to Eli to make him so desperately sad? What did Gideon do to him? What happened in London? Did I ever love someone that way? Did anybody ever love me? Was there someone out there who knew who I was? Was there somebody out there crying over me at that very moment? What was it like to love someone so very much the pain of his loss made you lose the will to live?

Lose the will to live. Realisation dawned with startling clarity. Eli wanted to die. He was starving himself to death, trying to turn himself to dust.

I flew up those stairs, quite literally. Through layers of

concrete, layers of marble, through Eli's empty bedroom rising through supporting beams and sheets of lead until I passed into the night above, into stars and moonlight.

I could not see him. Then I saw the flagpole, normally standing erect above the castle like a sentinel overlooking the valley, broken, jutting over the edge of the turret. My stomach churned with sickly dread as I edged toward the stone crenulation, unsure of what awaited me, unsure I wanted to see.

Sharp needles of bright light exploded above the distant tree line burning the image of the rising sun into my eyes. It felt more like Armageddon than a breaking dawn.

A rope dangled from the end of the pole, swinging taut in the gloom. The rope ended in a hangman's noose from which Eli hung lifeless.

The terror that surged through my being threatened to wipe me from existence — such was the feeling that engulfed me. I floated over to Eli, but his eyes remained tightly closed against me.

"Eli! Eli, please! Open your eyes!" Such was the hysteria in my voice that it reached a high-pitched squeal hitherto unknown. But his eyes did not flicker. I tried to touch him, but as always, my hands passed straight through him. My inability to make physical contact infuriated me and I clawed at him desperately, willing my flailing hands to touch solid flesh. Never had I been so desperate to touch something in all my life... or death... what use was I if I could not touch?

"Eli! Eli!" His eyes snapped open, emotionless and black.

"Leave me the fuck alone." His voice croaked as the rope cut into the flesh of his neck.

"For God's sakes, Eli, what are you doing?"

"Not for God's sake, you twat, for my sake! What does it look like I'm fucking doing? Piss off!"

I flew around him in a state of utter dismay. I did not know what to do or what to say. I stopped in front of him, so close to his face and yet so far from the man, staring into his dead eyes, eyes devoid of hope, devoid of life, devoid of reason. I saw the rising sun reflected in their watery depths and as the first warming rays began to touch his flesh, I felt overwhelmed by such a deep sadness that I could not help the tears that poured down my face.

"Eli, you do not deserve this." I was crying, I could not help it. "No one deserves to go through the pain you have suffered, but you cannot let this beat you, you are better than this."

"What do you know of my *suffering,* of my *pain?* Look at me, the sun is here and not even that will dare to touch my flesh."

Then his body exploded with sudden movement as his arms shot out and I flew backward, horrified by the violence of his flailing limbs. A shaft of bright light cut through the trees and bathed his body in a golden glow and I stared dumbfounded at the image blazing before me. Eli hung in grotesque cruciform and the scream that issued from his gaping mouth was a tortuous thing to hear, a painful cry into the heavens.

"Let me die! Why won't you let me die, you fucking cunt!"

Sharp fingernails whipped through the air, slicing effortlessly through the rope. With a backward flip, he landed on the downed flagpole and scampered along its length to disappear onto the roof.

I gave chase, but he had already disappeared into the depths of the castle. I sank through the layers of building, scanning each space for Eli as I plummeted through its depths until I finally found him standing in the hall. He had something in his hand and as I worked my way cautiously around, I saw with horror it was a paraffin lamp, its yellow flame flickering intensely.

"I can't even die. The sun won't touch me. Even that simple basic right is denied me." He brought the lamp up close to his face and I rushed forward, suddenly terrified. Flickering shadows danced across his already crazed face and the monster, the vampire, stared back at me from within.

"You cannot mean that, you cannot mean to die."

The creature before me cocked his head to one side. "Why should I not? I am but a curse on the face of this planet, a pestilence forced to feed on its lifeblood. I saved it once, and in return, it took away all that I loved, all that I believed in. I was with him for more than three hundred years. He found me, he helped me, he loved me, then he left me. Tell me, Malachi, how am I to live when all that I lived for is gone? How am I to live when my reason for living has been taken away from me? I know no life without Gideon, and life does not want to know me."

"Life needs you, I need you."

"Nobody will ever have that power over me again." To my relief he lifted the lamp to his lips and blew out the flame and his vampire face melted away. But the look in his eyes unnerved me, a cold unearthly stare that sawed through my soul with pitiless teeth then he spoke those words that broke my heart.

"I want you to leave."

I looked at him dumbfounded, feeling myself diminish beneath his gaze and I suddenly felt so very unimportant.

"What did you say?"

"I want you to leave, I do not want you here, I do not want to stare at your face and be constantly reminded. I don't want you in my life."

He meant it. The sincerity in his face told me that.

"But you need me..." Or was it I who needed him? All that time I thought I was helping him. I thought that deep down he needed me. I convinced myself he needed me when all the time it was the other way around.

"I don't need you." The words sliced through my heart and the pain of them rippled through my body. "I have *never* needed you. I want you to leave."

I stumbled toward him, my hands outstretched, pleading, begging him.

"But I need you, I love you..."

Such cruelty, he said each word with such cruelty, each word a dagger to my heart.

"But I *don't* love you. I can *never* love you. I will never love again."

Despite being dead, each word killed me. Each syllable, each letter, tore at the strands of my existence that tethered me to the world, evicting me from Alte, propelling me backward away from the man I loved.

The trees of the forest loomed above me. A tremendous force, a pull, a terrible sensation grew within me—I wanted to be sick. My body, my mind, it all meant nothing. The forest began to blur, trees melted before my eyes and the ground began to crumble beneath my feet.

I could not see Alte. I knew it was there, barely fifty yards away, but my eyes refused to see it, as though the image of my home, what I had come to think of as my home, no longer wanted me to see it.

How naïve to think that passing over would be easy. Where was my choir, my angels, where was my tunnel of welcoming light? Where was my God? But expectation withered beneath the pain of my body disassembling, of my molecules disseminating to the winds of the universe as so much useless dust. The loss felt profound and I was crying, my agony spilling down my cheeks in cruel rivers that dripped from my chin, carried away by the universe in disintegrating specks of nothingness.

I was unwanted. I was uninvited.

There came a voice, so distant and so faint I thought perhaps I imagined it. I could barely see, I could barely hear and any moment the world would cease to exist, or I would. The voice grew stronger, closer, the blackness that clouded my eyes flickered and I was so afraid if I moved I would blink out of existence, but all the time that voice taunted me, taunted me with the pretence of reality. It moved around me and I thought I glimpsed a shadow, a figure, shimmering through the edges of my own destruction and I wanted it to stop, just to let me go, to let it end.

A vision of such beauty appeared before me — my angel had arrived at last.

It was Eli.

The tone of his voice stunned me. Anger and bitterness had given Eli's tongue a vicious edge, but he stood there before me a contrite man, a desperate man, filled with regret, his words laden with remorse. Was that really the same mouth that only moments ago banished me from Alte?

Did my ears deceive me? Did the word *sorry* pass between his lips? Did the word even exist in his vocabulary?

"Malachi, please, I should not have said those things, and I didn't mean any of it. I'm sorry, Mal. Please believe that. Please forgive me. I open my mouth and crap falls out, you know what I'm like."

I had lived with the angry Eli for so long I could barely remember anything else, but he stood before me a man transformed.

"You said that you do not want me."

"That's not true, Mal, I know I said the words but they are not true. My anger, my frustration, I said those things in rage, mindless rage. I want you to come home, come home to Alte. Come home to me."

"But I do not have a home. Alte belongs to you, not me."

"Alte is not a home without you in it. I need you, Mal, I need your help, I need you to drag me back into the world of the living, but more than that, I need you to be my friend."

"I have tried to be your friend, but you push me away, you exclude me, and maybe I am better off just fading away..."

"That's me talking, not you. I am the defeatist. I am the one who has given up, lost hope. You have stayed by my side while I have been nothing but a selfish wanker obsessed with my own shit. I need you, I need your help."

"And you will talk to me?"

"Yes."

"And you will feed?"

"Yes!"

"And you will stop being a prize tosser?" I did not actually say the word *tosser*, but I was thinking it.

"I can't promise that, I'm arrogant by nature and vain by right... but I can promise I will try."

He had me at yes.

I made up my mind that day to change. As a spirit, I could not touch or influence anything around me. That had to change. So I practised. And that was how I came to find myself on a hill overlooking Welwelsburg death camp wearing the latest fashion in Germans. It was quite the full circle.

His name was Hans. And he was blond with blue eyes and a tan, a walking cliché of fit German manhood. I could feel him inside me... and not in a good way... a quiet presence I kept at bay. I could access his brain, simple as his brain might be, poor thing, but he did not have a clue about me and he felt nothing of the beating Eli had inflicted. There would be enough of that later, after I left.

If I left. I liked that body. I liked feeling the world around me. I liked *being*.

As I approached the gates, the area swarmed with soldiers and I felt sure a little bit of wee escaped. How delicious to be surrounded by so many handsome young men. Oh for a darkened room.

"Hans, where the fuck have you been?"

Okay, so he was not so cute. The man's face looked lop-sided and his nose bent awkwardly to the right. Still, he had lovely, eyes and I was a sucker for lovely eyes.

Was that concern I detected in his rough gravelly voice?

"I was attacked, runaways from the village, left me for dead."

"You'd better shift your ass to the infirmary and get yourself cleaned up before his Highness sees you."

"Oooo, royalty, I do so love a queen." My lips moved without thinking. He looked at me sideways, and it was not just because of the shape of his face.

"Our Blockfürher, you imbecile. The shit's hitting the fan and he's on the warpath, so come on, I'll take you to the infirmary and fill you in."

I beamed at my ugly friend while all the time I groped in Hans' head for his name. Stefan. That was his name. We had — that is Hans and Stefan had — grown up together, childhood friends, the same schools — joined the army together. More like brothers.

"Thanks. I could do with a cup of tea."

Stefan laughed as we ploughed through the throng of men and he punched me playfully on the arm. Hard. I squealed a little.

"Hans, you shit-face. Tea is for pansies! We will drink vodka."

I must have made a face because he stopped suddenly and grabbed me by the shoulders and stared intently into my face.

"How hard did those bastards hit you? You don't seem yourself."

I shrugged, suddenly very nervous.

"Well my head, it does hurt, and I do feel a bit woozy."

"What is the meaning of this?" Stefan suddenly stood to attention at the sight of a portly, rotund looking man. His uniform denoted a higher rank, so I desperately tried to give a convincing salute.

"Blockfürher. My apologies, I was just taking Hans here to the infirmary. He was attacked in the forest while hunting those Jewish bastards and I thought it best that he be checked over by the doc."

"You thought it best?" The round man glared at Stefan with sharp beady eyes and I actually found myself feeling sorry for him. "Since when did grunts like you think for themselves? Hmm? I asked you a question, private."

"Yes, sir. I mean no, sir, I think only what you tell me to think, sir."

The blob smirked, a disgusting, oily sensation. Then, to my horror, he cast his black piggy eyes over me and I felt a shiver of revulsion flush out my bowels. He frightened me so much that a little bit of wind escaped.

"Attacked, you say?" It was more of a statement than a question.

"Yes, sir. We ran into the forest after them, but I lost the others. I came upon a group of fugitives and I killed two of them, but they overpowered me and left me for dead. I woke up in a ditch and I could hardly breathe, I think they broke a couple of my ribs, and my head and legs are throbbing. I crawled back here on my hands and knees. I was so determined to get back... sir."

Both the Blockfürher and Stefan's eyebrows shot into the air with surprise and I could see Stefan was trying very hard not to laugh.

Suddenly the fat man let out a growl of what I took for laughter and slapped me on the shoulder. I nearly screamed with the pain and it was all I could do to stay on my feet.

"I like this one. But you killed two you say? Good. Come with me, both of you."

The Blockfürher led us back to the train where a torrent of wretched people were disembarking from cargo containers. Never had I seen such a mass of desperate looking faces. There were so many of them they could barely shuffle forward.

"These pathetic specimens, gentlemen, are the shit of human kind and we are tasked to deal with them."

A frail looking woman wrapped in a thin shawl fell to the floor.

The Blockfürher grabbed a rifle from a nearby soldier and thrust the rifle into my hands.

"You killed two, now kill another."

I stared at him in utter horror. He just grinned back at me, fat trembling lips salivating with anticipation. I wanted to throw up. The woman looked toward me and I could not bear to witness the hopeless desperation on her face.

I could have killed her. She was dying anyway. And the rifle felt so good in my hands, the hands that belonged to another, to the human I inhabited and it all felt so good. I could have stepped into that circle of disparate humans to feel the rush of their fear. I could have squeezed the trigger and put her out of her misery. No, I wanted to, I could feel it, the power of it, the overwhelming desire to extinguish her life.

I spun around, vomit flying from my mouth, the rifle held out away from me.

The fat man yanked the rifle out of my hand and thrust it into Stefan's arms. Stefan stiffened and walked forward into the crowd of prisoners until he was standing over the stricken woman, the muzzle of the rifle pointed at her head.

"Get up!" he screamed at her, but all she could do was look at him through dying eyes. Stefan kicked her body onto her back, then the rifle fired with a deafening bang and her head exploded across the soiled floor.

Without a word, without a look at the shattered body, Stefan made his way back to the Blockfürher and handed the weapon back to its owner.

"That is how you deal with the shit of humanity. Now take this vomiting fool from my site. And I want you both on box duty tomorrow."

Stefan froze and I could almost see the blood drain from his face. Poor bugger looked like he was about to faint. The Blockfürher stepped forward so his sweaty, wobbly features lay mere inches from Stefan's face.

"Is there a problem?" The threat underlying his words was unmistakable, poor Stefan.

"N-no, sir."

The Blockfürher moved in even closer, his repugnant lips brushing Stefan's ears.

"Get the fuck out of my sight."

Stefan tried to perform a salute that ended up more of an awkward stumble and he grabbed my arm and pulled me away. Even as we cut our way through the gawping crowd, I could feel the blob's piggy eyes burning into the backs of our necks.

I wanted to kill him. I wanted to rip his fat bulbous stomach open with my bare hands until his guts spilled hot and steaming onto the floor before me. Then I wanted to pick up his intestines and ram them down his throat until he choked on his own innards. The urge to turn and tear him apart burned right through my body to my fingertips. I could feel the heat rising in that body, feel its flesh prickle as the desire to kill, to maim, to inflict abject terror on my victim nearly overwhelmed me. It was all I could do to swallow down those impulses.

When we stood a fair distance from the gates, Stefan stopped me, his calloused hands gripping my shoulders roughly.

"Hans, do me a favour? The next time our Blockfürher tells you to shoot someone... fucking shoot them!"

"Really... there's no need to shout, old chap, is there any need?"

Stefan's hand flashed across my face, whipping my head back sharply.

"For fucks sake, Hans, get your pissing head in the game. Do you know how close you got to getting us shot, or worse?"

I rubbed my cheek. Hans was asleep deep inside me, his mind conditioned to feel no pain while I inhabited his body but I pretended all the same. At least I didn't have to feign surprise. Stefan's little outburst had truly shocked me and as I stared at the angry man glaring at me, I felt a little stirring down below. Yes, there was definitely something about him, he was ugly, but he could bend me over a tank any time. Stefan pushed me away with a sigh of exasperation and stalked off, shaking his head in disbelief. I had to power mince to catch up.

"Anyway, what could be worse than getting shot?"

"He could have us thrown to the boxes, that's what."

"And what the hell is box duty when it's at home?"

"For fucks sake, Hans. Have you lost your memories as well as your fucking mind?"

"I have been working, have I not? I've been in that awful village, running around forests, they beat me up! Really."

"The boxes, Hitler's dark army, his army of monsters, they are coming here. Himmler is on his way with trains full of them, hundreds of them. And those ghouls are coming with him, those... people from the Vril Society, they are all arriving here tomorrow and thanks to you, we are on box duty. We will have to cart those things off the trains, and if we are not careful, we will end up like those other poor bastards who pissed off the Blockfürher and were thrown to the boxes."

"What happened to them?"

"Dinner, that's what, drained them of every drop of their blood. There are monsters in those boxes, Hans, things out of your worst nightmare."

The creatures from Isaiah's diary were coming to Welwelsburg Camp, and Stefan said there were hundreds of them, hundreds of vampires. I had to warn Eli. An army of vampires, at Welwelsburg, the tall beings from Isaiah's youth. Himmler. More evil than you could shake a stick at.

I thrilled with excitement. And then I felt aghast that I should feel such a thing.

What the fuck was happening to me?

"What does Hitler want with an army of monsters in boxes anyway?" Stefan looked at me with horror and I realised then that I had spoken the question aloud instead of in my head as I had thought. Me and my lips.

"He's going to drop them like bombs on London. He controls them, all of them, I don't know how. Hitler is going to load them into buzz bombs and blitz London with an army of vampires."

Chapter Eighteen: Dead Camp Three

As related by Eli

Darkness still ruled supreme when the Kapo returned to wrench people callously from the shelves.

"Up, you filthy bastards, up. If you want to be fed then your beds will be made and you will be standing in line within the next ten minutes."

The Kapo reached my shelf, his dirty hand shot forward to seize the wrist of poor Jakob and I ripped the offending limb from my friend's dead flesh, being careful not to snap his greasy wrist. The thought of blood gushing from a gory stump, my hungry lips pressed flat against the dangling shards of flesh, my tongue guiding the warm fresh blood down my throat as his life emptied into me, pumped into me, flashed with alarming intensity through my head. Another time, another place and I would have been hard.

"He's dead!"

"Then you should be pleased. More room for you. The rubbish men will be here shortly, make sure you dispose of this crap." He looked at my hand wrapped tightly around his grotesque wrist. One flick and it would snap. One sharp pull would remove it from his person. Fucking twat deserved it.

Yet again, I amazed myself by demonstrating such uncharacteristic restraint.

"Touch me again and I will cut that hand from your limb." Begrudgingly I let go. He would keep.

Three prisoners had died in my block that night, two elderly and one young man not old enough to grow pubes. It sickened me. Never, in all my years, had I witnessed such a callous waste of human life. And then to see my fellow prisoners undressing the dead, striping their cold stiff bodies before my unbelieving eyes horrified me even more, and I clung onto Jakob's broken body for dear life. All around me the clunk of bodies against wood and concrete. My eyes tried not to see and my ears tried not to hear.

A cold clammy hand gently caressed my arm and I nearly shot off my shelf in shock. I didn't scream. I refused to scream.

"My friend, I'm sorry, my friend, but you must undress him. The rubbish men will be here soon and you must strip him of all clothing before they take him. Please, you must do this for him — they will be less kind than you. Do you understand?"

"Why? Why must we do this?"

"His clothes are of value, my friend. They will be re-used for the next intake."

"And what of his body, what will become of Jakob?"

"You don't want to know, my friend." His whispered words made every hair on my body stand on end. A sound outside caused him to return to his unsavoury task with renewed urgency. "Quickly, they are here."

What followed felt like a dream. I had undressed many a man under many circumstances, but that was a first. Already poor Jakob stiffened, and it pained me to hear and feel his bones crack as I gently prised his pale thin body from the clothes. I whispered my apologies into his unhearing ears and I hated my eyes for glancing across his pale dead flesh.

I had to free them, all of them. That place, that death camp, it had to end.

I lifted his dead naked body into my arms. Emotion, so

41

alien to me, invaded the shrivelled blackness that was my soul, and I knew my eyes betrayed my grief. Emotions made you weak. Emotions made you vulnerable, emotions hurt. And I was hurting. The passing of that human, that mortal man I had known for less than a day, had brought back that affliction from which I had been running from for so very long.

I had only opened my heart to the world again but for the briefest of moments. And already I felt pain.

Gideon hurt me. He made me feel unloved, unwanted, he made me feel ugly. How I would crave for his touch, how desperate I was for his love, to feel the thrill of his fingers upon my bare flesh, to feel his attraction to me, to feel wanted. But all he ever did was refuse me. Every time I tried to touch him, he turned me away. He was not in the mood, he told me to come back later.

Come back later.

But later never came.

I carried that pale body into the grey wet misery of morning. The sun was trying desperately to penetrate the thick layers of brooding clouds that clung stubbornly over the camp, but the sun was losing. Rain dripped incessantly from the skies, melting the remaining snow into a muddy slush. Grey skies, grey ground, grey people. The camp drained the colour out of everything. Welwelsburg was like me, a vampire, sucking the life out of everything it encountered, sucking away hope and dignity, leaving nothing but pale grey husks clinging to the brink of existence.

Two men stood next to a large flatbed trolley. Dead, naked bodies lay crumpled in a pile on top of the trolley, legs and arms sticking out at all angles like some grotesque starfish. I saw children amongst the corpses.

Pale white flickering figures surrounded the trolley.

Insubstantial wisps of lives spent before their time. The rubbish men looked at me expectantly but I could not move for the sight of those spectral beings and I clutched Jakob's dead body tightly to my chest, unwilling to relinquish my charge. If I put him on that trolley then he would be dead, another lump of cold meat on the pile. He deserved more than that.

The ghostly figures turned to look at me, each one knowing me, seeing me, seeing me see them. And they smiled at me. Cold shivering prickles erupted across my skin as their eyes took me in and they were such kind eyes, such trusting eyes. A figure pushed its way between them, its shadowy form brushing gently against the others as it came to stand before me.

Jakob looked into my astounded face and his gentle smile filled my dead body with something I could only describe as joy. The feeling was so strange to me that I barley recognised it. His eyes, so deep, so understanding, told me everything, that he was at peace, that he was where he belonged, that he would be okay. And it was such a relief to me, to know he felt at peace, to know his nightmare was finally over.

His hand passed gently across my cheek making my skin tingle.

He saw me for what I was, he saw the vampire. For the briefest of seconds, he seemed shocked as the truth of my being filled him, but then his eyes widened into circles of wonder as something akin to recognition dawned across his face and he laughed a joyous heart-warming thing that left me a little bemused. What else did he see in me? He looked at me with such knowing, such kindness, such awe and I wanted to see myself through his eyes, I wanted to see what he saw, perhaps the real me.

Then Jakob did something extraordinary. With such pride on his face, he took a couple of steps backward and used his fingers to make the sign of the cross across his chest, then he bowed. As he came back up his mouth moved, miming two silent words that for some inexplicable reason moved me to tears.

"Forgive him."

And then they faded, all of them, melting into the bitter cold.

The sudden sharp pain on the back of my leg shocked me back into reality and I saw the Kapo standing beside me slapping a vile looking whip in the palm of his hand. The fucking twat had slapped me with it. His sneering face loomed in closer to my face, and I could almost taste his perspiration.

"You waiting for a fucking bus or what? Move. Or would you rather face the hanging tree?" Saliva dribbled thickly from the corner of his mouth and his eyes glowed with feverish excitement. The corruption of power, there was nothing more frightening on the face of a human.

Gently, oh so very gently, I placed Jakob's corpse on the trolley and slowly and very deliberately, turned around to face the Kapo. His whip lashed out and cracked across my cheek with a snap. I could have stayed still, the assault was nothing to me, but I whipped my head back sharply and brought my hand up to cover my cheek. But he was not satisfied with my acting skills and he raised his arm in a wide swing, the whip flashing through the air for a second strike.

I reacted without thinking. Call it pride perhaps, or foolishness, or both, but I would not let that disgusting piece of shit masquerading as a human strike me a second time. My hand streaked out with lightning speed and snatched the whip from his hand before it had the chance to reach its full downward arc and I snapped it in half with my fingers. The pieces fell useless to the floor.

There was a collective gasp of astonishment. People parted like the red sea. Whether it was my lightening reflexes or my insubordination that produced the reaction I would never know, but as the Kapo's astounded face turned to undiluted rage, I knew I had gone too far.

The sight of his face turning such a bright purple-red would have amused me under any other circumstance. Seldom had I seen a human change colour in such a spectacular fashion. Like a Charlie Chaplin comedy, I could almost see the steam spurting from his ears in horizontal jets. Stupid fucking twat.

"Den Baum Hängen! Den Baum Hängen!" It was an impressive hissy fit.

All of a sudden, a fist shot out from nowhere and the Kapo fell into a sprawling heap on the floor. The look on his face was priceless. He was about to launch into a fresh tirade when he saw who it was that knocked him so unceremoniously onto his ass.

The Blockfürher stared down at the little man, his nostrils flaring, and I tried very hard not to let my face register the deep felt satisfaction that threatened to spread across it. I had to bite the insides of my lips to stop myself from laughing.

"Put him to work! Do you know who is coming tomorrow? Do you?" The Kapo cringed beneath his booming voice.

The corners of my mouth twitched. I could taste my own blood.

"Yes, sir. Yes, sir!"

"Then I suggest that if you do not want to be thrown to the boxes, you feed these worthless bags of piss and put them to work immediately. Do I make myself quite clear?"

"Yes, sir. Of course, sir!"

"Then get up!" He kicked the Kapo violently in his side.

That made me wince, I could almost feel the pain shooting through the Kapo's kidney.

I felt no sympathy, just satisfaction.

Without missing a beat, the Blockfürher swung around to face me, his fat podgy face wobbling inches from my own. I would never have attributed such pirouetting grace with the likes of something so grotesquely fat. And his breath stank, garlic sausage and pickled cabbage. Black beady eyes glanced down with utter disdain at my yellow Star of David glowing proudly on my chest.

"Fucking Jew. This thieving piece of shit," and he stabbed me in the chest repeatedly with a sausage finger, "you may hang him by the hands, after the work is done." Without a second glance toward me, he pushed past, his scampering, squirming entourage flagellating themselves in his shadow.

"Get in line, you fucking worthless pig. Move!" The Kapo bellowed the command, but there was no conviction in his voice.

I trudged toward the line of grey inmates through grey mud under a grey sky. The atmosphere weighed on me heavily and it carried with it a feeling of despondency that made the burden almost unbearable. Every face around me wore the same desperate look, hopelessness.

I wanted out of there. I wanted and needed to be away from that pit of human depravity. I wanted to crawl back to my castle and wrap myself in the biggest most comfortable blanket I could find and never venture into God's forsaken world again.

God's forsaken world, wasn't that a fucking fact, for surely God had forsaken the world and all the poor bastards that inhabited it. What god would allow such things to happen? What god would allow his creations to treat each other so? God, in his infinite wisdom created vampires, demons, The Mother, The Father and God created humans,

the scariest motherfuckers of them all. We are all
perversions, vampire, demon, ghost, and human—it just
boiled down to scale.

Why did I remain in that cesspit? Why was I there?

Ethan. It was all for Ethan, the human, the flesh and
blood, fragile and ephemeral Ethan. All humans were the
same, but not all humans were Ethan. Was Ethan more than
human? The familiarity of him stuck to me like a half formed
memory, clawing at me with intangible fingers. From the
moment I pulled him out of the mud, I knew it, I knew him.
I felt him.

I was doing it for Ethan. And I was doing it for every
wretched human in that stinking, wretched place.

Breakfast, if you could call it that, consisted of a chunk of
dry bread and a tin can filled with a noxious brown liquid
laughingly called coffee. As a vampire, I did not need to eat
human food, but the joys of good cuisine often satiated my
desires when sex was otherwise unavailable. Food or wank?
More often than not, food won over. My body did not
absorb solid food in the same way as a human, and the
result was that it felt like the whole world was falling out of
my ass. It came out the same way it went in, not an attractive
sight. Imagine trying to pass an entire roast chicken dinner—
nasty.

The thought of eating with so many hungry faces
surrounding me just felt wrong, so I gave my bread to the
ghost of a man standing next to me, the one who tipped me
off about the bin men. He looked at me gone off.

"Go on, please, take it, you need it more than I do." I
thrust the thankless chunk of edible rock into hands that
shook with eagerness. "What's your name?"

"Marni, my name is Marni," he spluttered between
grateful mouthfuls.

"I am Eli."

"Ascension." I looked at him strangely and he laughed, crumbs hitting my flesh like bullets. "Your name, it means ascension in old Hebrew."

"Well, you learn something new every day. Thank you for that revelation."

"Kind of a hobby of mine, names, their meaning. You can learn a lot from a name. I think my mother must have had a funny turn when she named me. Marni is old Hebrew for rejoice. Rejoice I tell you. She saw things, my mum, always said that one day I would live up to my name. Funny how things turn out."

Poor man, he certainly had nothing to rejoice about sitting in that camp.

"Mind you, you're one lucky son of a bitch though, aren't ya? Lucky to be standing here at all. Don't think I've ever seen anyone stand up to the Kapo before—and stay alive that is."

"What's with this hanging tree thing anyway?"

"Den Baum Hängen? It's a particularly nasty form of punishment. They tie the offender's hands behind his back then hang him from a post by the hands. Your arms are dislocated and you are left there until you die."

"The sick fucks."

"Stay alive long enough and you will see much worse, I guarantee it."

"The boxes?"

I did not think it possible for him to pale any further, but he did. I could almost see his body shiver and diminish at the very mention of the boxes.

"I've never seen them. I spent most of my captivity in the factories building rockets. But I've heard of them, and if they are coming here you can kiss your ass goodbye."

"But what's in the boxes?" Like I didn't already know, but I needed to hear it, from someone alive, someone other than the pages of an Exorcising super Rabbi.

"What's in the boxes? No one has seen, no one alive that is. But I will tell you one thing, wherever those boxes go, people disappear, and there is always more boxes that leave a place than arrives in a place. Now make of that what you will, but those boxes are an omen, and if the Vril Society is bringing them here then you can bet there is nothing Godly in them."

And there was my confirmation, the old enemy. My head exploded with sudden pain and I thought I would go blind from the sheer panic that crashed over me, real, tangible, gut wrenching fear that nearly split my mind from my skull. The Vril Society, an occult elitist group hell bent on destroying mankind. And if they were coming to Welwelsburg, that meant the Thul, their leaders, my enemy, would be close. There were two worlds colliding inexorably before my eyes, my past that I had tried so hard to suppress and my present, which I was trying so hard to survive and all of it leading to one thing, a great big pile of steaming shit.

It was always going to happen. I was stupid to think otherwise, to think I could hide from them, to presume that I could wipe my hands clean of London and never face those bastards again — the inevitability of it smacked me across the face with a brick, and fuck did it smart. They were as much a part of my existence as the blood I needed to survive.

I cursed Isaiah and I cursed his damn book. I knew when I read it, I felt them looking back at me from the pages of that book, taunting me, seeing me, letting me know I had been found. All of history infected by their evil, and they had infected me with their poison, rotting my existence from the inside, eating away at my sanity with greedy mouths, devouring my life bit by bit until there was nothing left but shit, loneliness and guilt. I should have ended it then when I was at my lowest, when London took all that I had and consumed all that I was. But I was a coward, I did not have the guts to take that relic, that splinter, to plunge it into my stone cold heart and end my existence as I had with Morbius.

An ice-cold chill rippled down my spine at the very thought of his name. Morbius, the supreme ruler of the Thule, a demon, a creature of pure hatred and darkness, older than mankind, a Menarche of such exquisite evil, and I had killed him. The Thule were scattered, the Vril Society plunged into chaos without their ruling body. And I escaped with nothing. They took it all from me. I lost Gideon. I lost my capacity to love, my capacity to care. I lost any hope of my own humanity.

Now they were coming to Welwelsburg, the Thule, the Vril, ancient and cunning, utterly remorseless, back into my life once again.

I was shaken from my thoughts of impending shittyness as the Kapo marched us brusquely and in deathly silence toward the fenced off area with its mounds of discarded clothing. A huge fire burned in the middle of the enclosure and through the thick putrid smoke that coiled like some vast Kraken above our heads, I could see pale grey figures feeding the fire with great handfuls of cloth.

"This area is to be cleared immediately. You will not go back to your bunker until this work has been completed, is that understood?"

Mountains of clothes, my mind could not grasp the scale of what my eyes witnessed. Daylight revealed a mountainous sea of them, thousands of discarded garments, thousands of them.

The smoke made the task unbearable. The acrid fumes of burning fabrics stung our eyes, and rain mingled with ash to streak our pale faces. We worked in silence, heaving armfuls of heavy wet garments, tossing them into the enormous bonfire that blazed fiercely at the heart of the enclosure. Some of the men had long rake-like implements that they plunged into the heart of the pyre, stoking the flames higher so they leaped defiantly into the dripping grey sky. Vampires and fire are not happy bedfellows, and the heat radiating from that burning pit made my skin crawl.

Perhaps the worst part of it for me was the smell. I had heightened eyesight, heightened hearing, heightened strength and a heightened sense of smell, heightened everything really, and all around me the smell of a thousand souls. Every armful of clothing I carried filled my nostrils with the smell of forgotten lives. The lingering smell of lavender soap, of medicated shampoo, of shattered dreams and half-glimpsed nightmares and all interspersed with the ubiquitous stench of urine and shit. However, there was something else lingering amid the fibres of lost lives, a scent that to me was all too familiar — terror. When a human feels fear, fear that raises the hair on the back of the neck, terror that runs thickly down your legs, it leaks out into the sweat, an aroma quite distinct and instantly recognisable to any vampire. We smell it during the hunt, when the victim finally realises what it is that stalks them, what it is that is eating them. It floods their bloodstream and leaks out of every pore. It was intoxicating to us. The clothing reeked of terror.

"Hark at you doing manual labour."

It was Mal. I gave him one of my best withering looks, but my expression quickly softened when I looked into his badly bruised face. His features displayed a criss-cross of sutures and tape, but he looked a lot better than when I last saw him.

"And hark at you, inside a man, again."

"Oooo, touchy aren't we?"

"What are you doing here, Mal? You're supposed to be

up at the castle looking for Isaiah."

Mal scooped up an armful of clothes. He moved differently somehow, more manly, as though the body he inhabited owned him. It unnerved me. The possession could not last much longer, for both Mal's sake and the human's.

I almost laughed as his nose wrinkled up at the foul smell.

"Yeah, well, we mere grunts have been put to work to help you lot clear this area before tomorrow morning."

"That's when the boxes are arriving."

Mal looked surprised. "Yes. How in hell did you know that? I couldn't wait to get here to tell you. Isaiah's boxes are coming here."

The flames hissed and sent spirals of sparks and black fumes into the sky as we threw our loads into the furnace.

"And that's not all that's coming. The Thule, those creatures from the book, they are coming to Welwelsburg Castle. Something big is going down."

"You're telling me. Hitler wants to drop vampires on London using buzz bombs."

I felt my face hit the floor, my jaw literally dislocating to bury itself in the mud at my feet. As far as plans went, that was by far the most audacious thing I had ever heard. My God, the scale of it, to rain such death down from the sky, to unleash hordes of feral vampires across a city already shattered by uncompromising war. It would be like the Black Death all over again. A virile disease spreading outward from London exponentially, consuming every town, every borough until Great Britain was nothing but an island of living dead.

And once Britain fell, what then? America? Russia? All the world's great continents reduced to mindless blood sucking monsters. A world consumed by the never-ending need to devour blood.

But what was the point? What was the motive for creating

such an army, an army of swarming, feeding, merciless monsters who would do nothing but feed until there was nothing left to feed on? There would be nothing left. The earth wiped clean of humanity with nothing but a handful of immortal Menarche to populate a dead world. And what was the point in that? The entire concept was a massive affront to God.

"When? When does this happen."

"I don't know."

"Then for fucks sake get back to that castle and let me know when you have something useful to tell me!" I regretted my anger instantly. My own fears and horrors were leaching out, infecting my words, infecting my reason and Mal did not deserve the vitriol that dripped from my ungrateful lips.

I looked into his face expecting to see hurt and perhaps a pout, but what I saw there froze my apology to my lips. Anger transformed the soldier's features into a caricature of humanity as the darkness took control, eyes blazing with fury, eyes that glowed yellow.

Possession fit. The longer he stayed in that body, the more his soul disintegrated and soon the rage would consume every ounce of that which was once Mal until there was nothing left but a demon. I could see the battle all over his face, throughout his trembling body as he tried to control the fury that burned in his blood. He clenched and unclenched his fists so tightly I could smell the blood welling up in the palms of his hands.

"Malachi, listen to me, you must calm yourself, concentrate, don't let the anger take you over, remember who you are... remember why we are here." My words meant nothing to him as he advanced toward me, hands balled into angry fists. I was in trouble. We both were.

Over his shoulder I could see two Nazi troops

approaching, attracted by the prospect of a fight. Without hesitation, I launched myself into Mal's arms and whispered urgently into his tortured face.

"Beat the fucking crap out of me. Now!"

As my words penetrated his demon crazed skull, I saw the fit begin to slip away. Tormented yellow eyes flickered between monstrous rage and human desperation as glimpses of the true Mal fought to regain supremacy. I needed to shock him back into reality and I needed his actions to convince the approaching troops that there was nothing for them to see.

"Fucking hit me, Mal!"

With effortless power and a howl of fierce rage, he threw me to the floor and pushed my face into the muddy quagmire beneath my body. Suddenly his foot flashed out and connected with my rib cage with a deafening bang. My ribs shattered. I felt them pop and splinter inside me.

His eyes blazed so yellow, fiercer than any flame, threatening to consume us both with their incandescent rage. Malice transformed his face to wipe away the human and a smile flashed across his features, a smile so wide it nearly split his head in two. It was a look of pure pleasure, a smile of relish and I wept inwardly at the realisation that he was enjoying himself.

With a thunderous crack, his foot hit my chest for a second time and I could barely hold onto consciousness as agony exploded through my body. My breath gushed from my chest in a great painful whoosh as ribs, already shattered, ripped through my lungs.

A scream ripped itself painfully from between my lips making him hesitate, just for a second. For that briefest moment of time, I saw his old face, my friend's face, Mal's face, glimmering through the human flesh of the soldier. It was a face filled with horror. It was a face crying out for forgiveness, so desperate and pleading, frightened.

Conflict morphed his flesh between human and demon and as I lay there, shattered and broken, I prayed to my friend to fight.

A scream forced its way through his pursed lips. His head arched back sharply, his arms rigid at his sides as demon and ghost fought over the host's body.

The two soldiers ran toward us, their rifles raised. We had seconds left.

"Mal, please," I said between clenched teeth. My entire chest area moved beneath my clothing as my ribcage healed, like a thousand fingers crawling beneath my skin and the sensation was both unnerving and intensely painful. I could not let the soldiers see me healing. I extended a claw and cut into the flesh of my face until a fountain of blood cascaded across my skin and clothes. I rubbed the red fountain all over my face and hands incorporating as much mud into the mix as I could until I looked the part of the beaten prisoner. What goes around comes around. The irony of it did not escape me.

"For fucks sake, Mal, hit me, hit me!"

Mal's head snapped back to normality as the possession fit died. He looked down at me with such pain, such guilt and self-loathing and it was all I could do not to cradle him in my arms and tell him it was okay, that it was not his fault.

It was my fault. I had put him through that hell. He stood shocked and distraught before me, yet another monster of my own making to add to my growing list.

"I'm sorry." A single tear spilling from his pleading eyes. His hand lashed out and collided with my bloodied face and I flung myself backward against the earth with as much conviction as possible, just as the soldiers reached our position.

"What's up? He giving you trouble?"

"Nothing I can't handle." The manliness of Mal's voice surprised me. Then he snorted. The vile, wet sound went up his nose and into his mouth. He spat, the thick glutinous contents of his nasal passages hitting my face, sliding across my mouth. The action was so unexpected and so butch I nearly laughed, but that would have meant opening my mouth and swallowing the gob, not.

"Cock sucking cunt!" I pretended to shrink away from Mal in fear, burying my face in my arms, a move designed to hide my smirk as much as to convince them of my fear.

Suddenly, I felt two pairs of hands grip me by the shoulders and drag me across the muddy floor. I briefly saw a look of confusion cross Mal's face, replaced by a look of absolute horror as he realised what his comrades intended.

They were dragging me toward the fire.

Fire would not kill me. Fire would burn away my flesh and blacken my bones. But I would still be alive and I would feel everything, the pain unimaginable. My brain would recognise the sensation of skin and muscle dripping away from bone, recognise the explosions inside my chest as my lungs expanded and burst. And even as they left me desiccated and wasted, my brain would continue to tell me I was alive, continue to feed me the agony of combustion.

And then the regeneration would start. New muscle and new skin would wrap itself around my blackened skeleton, making me anew. And it would happen quickly. And it would happen in front of my captors.

I tried to scramble backward as the heat of the approaching furnace toyed with my flesh, careful to conceal my strength, careful to conceal my vampire. I heard Mal's panicked voice, his frantic shuffle as he struggled to pull away one of my assailants. Yet, all I could see was the fire looming closer, all I could feel was the searing heat eager to cook my skin.

The smack of a hand against human flesh halted the struggle and one of the soldiers fell to the floor. He looked up at Mal, a look of shocked outrage on his bruised face.

"You fucking twat, what was that for? We're only having a bit of fun."

"And it will be my ass that will be fucked if you kill him before this shit of a job is finished. Do you want the Blockfürher to throw you to the boxes? Cause I fucking don't."

The soldier on the floor glanced up at his comrade nervously. Mal reached out and helped him off the floor. He clamped his arm around the stunned soldiers shoulder in a gruff, manly, no hard feelings kind of way.

"I can handle this bag of shit—go back to your posts before someone notices you've left them." That seemed to do the trick and both men scurried away, the one rubbing his cheek sorely.

"And you, you fucking Jewish cunt, back to work before I change my mind!" He yanked me roughly from the floor and pulled me close to his snarling face.

"Always remember I love you," he whispered and then, flinging me violently onto the ground, he turned his back and marched away.

His parting statement shook me, and not for the first time, I thought his affection undeserved. As I gazed at his back, at his sad slumped shoulders, an overwhelming wave of sorrow hit me because I knew, without any doubt, that things would never be the same between us. The Mal I knew, the Mal I loved, the Mal who made me laugh and who infuriated me, would not leave Welwelsburg the same creature that had entered. It had to be that way, because when our ordeal was over, I was going to break his heart.

It was my fault, all of it. There was a demon taking root in his soul, my fault. It was my idea, the possession, beating his host to a pulp, all of it, my fault. And he was doing it for me and I let him, my fault, all of it my fault. And the worst of it was I knew he would. I knew he would do anything for me. And that made me the most despicable monster of them all.

I was running out of time. I had to get Malachi out of Welwelsburg and out of that body before it was too late.

But they were coming, the boxes, the Thule. Maria and Klingsor, or The Mother and The Father as I knew them, they were coming. There was nowhere to hide any more. They were coming, and I was afraid.

Chapter Nineteen: Dead Camp Four

As related by Malachi

I left him on the floor. I left the man I loved cowering on the floor covered in his own blood. The man I said no to an angel for. The man I had beaten to a pulp. The man I *enjoyed* beating to a pulp.

I didn't understand what was happening to me. As I walked away from my shattered friend, I could still feel the anger, the undiluted rage surging through my blood stream, through my host's bloodstream, giving me strength, giving me power, wooing me.

Some part of me wanted it. Some part of me welcomed the anger, welcomed the power that made me his equal. I saw the fear that flickered across Eli's face as my boot met his firm hard body. I saw the shock on his gorgeous face as his ribcage shattered at my touch. I felt the crunch of bones through my thick leather boot, rippling up my leg into my groin, stirring the cock of the walking sack of meat I inhabited. It excited me. I could still feel the dampness of my host's ejaculation against his skin, against my skin.

Against *my* skin.

And I enjoyed it. I enjoyed watching that smug faggot bastard writhing on the floor in agony. I enjoyed watching Eli cringe away from *me*, from *my* power, from the pain that *I* inflicted.

That was so not me. I would rather cut off my left tit than cause him pain.

It didn't feel like me when I was doing it. Oh, I knew it was, I could see myself lashing out and breaking bones, but at the same time, I felt removed from my actions, on the outside looking in. It was a different kind of Malachi. A Malachi that felt emboldened, empowered, a Malachi with no inhibitions. I was becoming more than just a disembodied sex deprived floating orgasm. My mind felt clear, un-clouded by thoughts of unrequited love, uncomplicated by the meaning of my existence. It was my destiny. To be powerful, to be strong, to be a thing respected, a thing feared. In that sublime moment, confidence coursed through my veins like electricity, together with the certain knowledge that I was untouchable, a God in the making.

I was the one with the power. *I* was the one who was irresistible. *I* was the one loved.

From where that feeling of love originated I did not know. It was there, lurking around the periphery of my consciousness, the feeling of something loving me, of wanting me, of desiring me. And I knew it without question. I knew I was all of those things, given to me freely and unconditionally. I deserved them and they were there for the taking. Love that burned, love that filled every sinew of my being. Desire that satisfied me beyond the realms of what I ever thought possible, irresistible, intoxicating and all for me.

And then I was back. The strength, the power, the love, snatched away from me without thought or consideration, leaving me empty, lonely, a useless shell. Without warning, without mercy, it pulled itself out of my head, sucking away my humanity, an agonising withdrawal that left me... normal. It felt like I would never know happiness again, or love, or sexual gratification. It left me drained and pathetic. All I could feel was anger, anger that such a sensation should be denied to me, and I wanted it to come back. I was desperate for it to come back, to fill me with its rapture, to drown me in its ecstasy.

Was that corruption, I wondered? Was that how it felt to become a demon? I knew the risk. Eli, the angel, they knew it could happen, but I did it all the same. The thing inside me would grow and grow until there was nothing left of me, nothing left but burning hatred, a demon.

But I still said yes.

But my soul belonged to me and was mine to risk and mine to give. And I would give it to him gladly, to my Eli, for my Eli. I risked my soul for him and him alone, not for Ethan, not for Isaiah, not because there were monsters in uniform to overthrow but because *he* needed me to do it. Eli needed me and I would risk everything, always, just for him.

I wanted to cry.

I felt weak, ashamed, brittle, thinned out to the point of disappearing, on the edge of some catastrophic emotional collapse. I had the flair for the dramatic and I intended to use it.

I could feel hot tears in my eyes as my soldier's vision blurred and I could feel his lips trembling, the blood rushing to his cheeks. My breakdown cometh and not even the hordes of Hell could prevent it.

I could not allow anyone to see me in that state, so I ducked into the nearest building, a large concrete block with a tall chimney belching forth thick plumes of black smoke. No sooner had I slammed the door behind me than my body started to convulse as great heaving sobs shook my shoulders and reduced my legs to quivering jelly. I leaned against the inside wall, hands clawing at my face in desperation as I fell apart. The wails that escaped through my clenched teeth issued from another man's throat, another man's voice, but it was with my despair, my torment that I ripped and pulled at my hair and flesh.

If the angel had stood before me in that moment, I would have said yes.

"Are you okay, sir?" The voice was weak, timid and it scared the hell out me.

It took my tear-frosted eyes a few seconds to blink away the film of hysteria that clogged them with a haze of grief and then a few seconds more for my eyes to adjust to the oppressive gloom that surrounded me.

Fuck me pink it was hot in there.

A hand touched my elbow. I freaked out, a loud girly scream escaping from my disobedient lips, a sound so high pitched as to summon dogs, and I lashed out quickly to dispel the offending limb.

"Get your fucking hand off me!" It was a vain attempt to regain my manhood but no matter how hard I tried, the voice box of my host still managed to convey an innate campness. How very rude.

He was a ragged creature and very young, painfully so, and he was covered in sweat, his cloths plastered to his body. I could see the outline of his ribs jutting through the thin striped uniform. Black soot smeared his incredibly chiselled face and I found myself wondering how glorious a figure he would present given different circumstances.

I couldn't help it. He was cute.

"What the fuck are you doing here?" I barked with as much authority as I could muster. He cringed away from me, utterly terrified. I had to remember what I was wearing. Of course, he was terrified.

"I'm on rubbish duty, sir, this is the recycling room."

The boy, for surely he was no more than nineteen, stepped aside and I wished at that moment I were blind. For the love of God, I wanted someone to tear out my offended eyes.

I wanted to be sick. I gripped my knees, frightened that

they would crumble from beneath me. Bile and chunks of breakfast filled my tightly closed mouth and I had no choice but to swallow the lumps. If I opened my mouth, I didn't know if the screaming would stop.

Set into the back wall of the brick lined torture chamber sat a huge furnace, its gaping mouth belching fierce orange flame that flickered across the back wall as though it were alive, squirming and undulating in some vile hope of escape. Even from my viewpoint by the door, I could see the burned remains of the corpses lying within, crumbling beneath the onslaught of the white-hot inferno. Blackened skulls leered at me, taunting me, daring me to scream. Angry, flame licked mouths bellowed their innocence in a cacophony of spent agony.

In front of the Hell mouth and just to the right sat a flatbed trolley laden down with a cargo that carried the last of my sanity into the ether. Pale white skeletal bodies lay piled one on top of the other in a tortured tapestry of distorted limbs. It was a monstrous sculpture of discarded, wasted lives.

It started again, that feeling deep within, of the demon, my embryonic demon, stirring, awakening, desperate to consume and become me. I felt my anger, my rage begin to swell, my arms moving involuntarily, my fingers extending into sharp talons, the feel of flesh and muscle and fragile bone so good beneath my skin. I could snap the boys throat in an instant, a mere second of strength, all it would require was a simple twitch, a flick of my wrist and he would cease to exist and my demon would have the soul it so badly desired. Dust exploded into my face as his back slammed into the brick wall behind him, held there by a hand I could not control, that I did not want to control.

What was that look I saw upon his face? Was it terror? My demon loved terror. Was it the final realisation he was about to die? My demon loved death.

No. It was neither. My demon would have neither.

Was that resignation my demon saw in his eyes? Yes, but it was more than that. Those tears, the wetness that fell so freely down his sallow face from eyes that glittered green but had no life. My demon knew that look, knew that it would come up empty handed, that it would have to wait, that its time was yet to come. I felt my demon wither, vanquished by that look, the look of relief, of release.

"Please kill me." His voice, so impassioned, broke what little heart I had left.

"Do not ask that of me," I implored, suddenly terrified of what I might do. I let go of his throat and he slumped to the floor, coughing and spluttering. I went to turn away from him, but a feeble hand gripped my ankle. He was at his wits end, his face a torment of utter desperation.

"Please, I'm begging you." Spittle dribbling thickly from the corner of his cracked lips. "Put me out of my misery, I won't do this anymore... I can't do this anymore." His last words drowned in the sobs that ripped his soul apart.

The horror of that room was not his fault. It was not of his doing. He was only acting under instruction, forced to do unspeakable things.

He did not kill them did he?

He was just doing his job, wasn't he?

As they were all doing their job, following orders, every last fucking one of them.

I kicked his hand away from my foot, more viciously than I intended. I did not want to be cruel, but I would not be his judge or executioner.

His gaze bore into me. God those eyes, the pleading behind them, the soul yearning for release from such interminable suffering, a man, no, a boy, his humanity exposed with nothing left but death.

"You make me burn them, you make me bring them here, my friends, and you make me burn them. You call them rubbish, and they were my friends." I heard no malice, no hint of accusation in his broken voice, just raw naked pain, a sharp reminder of the thing I wore.

I didn't know what horrified me the most, the fact that I had nearly killed him or the fact that the young man had been pushed so far that all he wanted was death. It made me think of Eli, and I thought then, perhaps for the first time, that I finally understood.

He was just another innocent victim, as dead as those corpses he fed into the furnace.

Something shivered down my spine. Icy fingers dug into my vertebrae, alerting me, warning me, teasing me with the promise of more horror yet to come. My hair stood on end and the skin I wore goose pimpled.

And then I saw them, dozens of them.

They stood with their faces against the wall around the perimeter of the building, ghostly figures dressed in the all too familiar black and white uniforms in which they died.

"Get out of here." I couldn't look at him as he cowered away from me. I couldn't tear my eyes away from the queue of spectral beings.

A shaft of white light made me wince and I turned just in time to see the boy's back slip through the crack of the door.

"This is almost over!" I shouted after him, trying to make my words seem as reassuring and encouraging as possible. "Don't give up, you will get out of this, I promise you!" It was all I could offer him. He glanced back, just the once, all confusion and hopelessness. How weird that must have been for him, to hear a Nazi speak those words of comfort. After all, that was all he could see, just another monster in a uniform.

It was the first time I had been so close to a ghost, never

mind so many of them. Strange, I know, but I had spent so long in my insulated Eli world that I knew nothing else. It had always been just the two of us. I had spotted the occasional apparition over the years, fleeting glimpses through the trees surrounding Alte, and I even chased after one once. I cried out for it to stop, to stay and talk with me a while, to tell me about its death, its life, in the vain hope that I would learn a little about my own in return. Did we have anything in common? Did he remember his life, how he died? But they never seemed to want to talk to me.

Just like a man, always looking for something better.

For some reason, I thought I could touch one. They looked so solid. My hand shook as I reached out to touch the first ghostly figure. I really wanted to feel it, to make a connection with it—I *needed* to feel connected to it.

"Please, who are you?" My voice sounded so whiny and I hated the neediness that infected my words.

Suddenly the ghost began to bang its head against the brick wall. It should not have made a sound—I should not have been able to hear the slap, slap of flesh hitting stone and I should not have been able to see blood spray out across the walls in front of it with every beat of its head. But I could hear it. I could almost *feel* it.

I recoiled in horror. Then the ghost next to him began to do the same then the next and so on until the whole room filled with the wet slap of bloodied flesh against brick.

"What are you doing?" Bang, bang, bang, slap, slap, slap. The sound was nauseating.

"Stop it. Stop it!"

With calculated unity, each ghost raised their hands and placed them against the wall, shoulder width apart. Bang, slap, blood sprayed thickly across fingers and wrists.

"Why won't you talk to me?" I ran along the line of self-immolating figures, my voice rising with hysteria as I screamed at their unresponsive backs. But they would not stop and they would not face me.

My rage and frustration gushed up my throat shredding my lungs.

"Talk to me!"

The head banging stopped.

"Ever heard the expression *hitting your head against a brick wall?*"

I spun around, almost falling over my own feet at the sound of the voice behind me. He was standing in the middle of the room, hands clasped before him, wearing a perfectly tailored black suit cut against his frame in all the right places. The bulge squeezing through his tightly fitted trousers looked positively obscene. Jet-black hair sat slicked back across his scalp. A crisp, blindingly white shirt housed an elegant black silk tie, and I nearly drowned in his beautiful yellow eyes, yellow eyes that glittered from within a stunningly cherubic face. And he was wearing spats. I nearly creamed my pants.

"Who the hell are you?" A simple question I thought, but he laughed all the same.

"Dear heart, do you really need me to tell you?"

My God, that voice, it made my skin erupt with goose flesh, made my body tingle—he was so magnetic. He reminded me so much of that handsome angel.

The penny dropped, as did my jaw.

"Fuck me!"

He sashayed toward me in long elegant strides, a smirk pasted across his beautiful face. I could not move, not out of fear but because I did not want to. I did not want to move away from him, even when he reached out a slender arm and reached down between my legs to grip my stiffened cock.

"Yes." He moved his lips against my ear, his breath hot

against my skin. "If you wish. You can call me Melek." I wriggled away from him, covering my bulge with shame, but he laughed a toying, playful sound that told me my reticence was but a half-felt gesture.

"They will not talk to you, dear heart," he said, extending his arm out like a ballerina, all elegance and poise, to point at the ghosts. I had almost forgotten their presence.

"Why?"

"Because they are ashamed of you, my poor deluded little child, surely you know that?"

My head reeled. What had I done to deserve such derision?

"But why, for what possible reason?" He turned back to face me and somehow his fingers caressed my cheek, despite him standing on the opposite side of the room. It made me shudder.

"Because of what you have done to that body, dear heart."

"I have done no such thing!"

"What? Not even just a little bit? Just a little touch? A fondle?"

My face, or rather my soldier's face, burned red with humiliation.

"I thought as much. Oh please... do not think that I judge you, who am I to criticise?"

"You're telling me they are ashamed of me because I like men?" The anger flared inside me and I could feel my demon rubbing its clawed hands against my flesh with glee.

"You might well think that, but I couldn't possibly comment."

"I'm not ashamed of what I am!" I stared him down, unflinching, defiant.

"There he is," he beamed, "my little devil!" He turned to the ghosts, suddenly serious. "Turn around." The commanding tone of his voice was irresistible. One by one the ghosts turned, their faces a bloody mess of flayed skin and bone.

"Look at them," said Melek with surprising kindness. "Look properly, dear heart, what do you see?"

The blood disappeared, raw flesh healed and I stared into a dozen faces young and old, everyday faces of everyday people. Each wore the same striped uniform, the pyjamas as the Nazi soldiers called them, and each had a badge on their chest.

The badges, they were all the same, pink triangles, every one of them. They were all convicted homosexuals. I turned around angry, my eyes blazing with fury and disgust.

"Do not look at me like that, Malachi. You made this about sexuality, not me. Let others play that card, but do not, for one minute, deal it to me!"

"But you said they were ashamed of me... you made me think..."

"No, you made yourself think. Do not ever be ashamed of who or what you are, dear heart, embrace everything you are, for you are beautiful."

"Then why? Why are they ashamed of me?" Even my lips blushed.

"In their eyes you are an abomination. You are a spirit who has taken possession of a human body, corrupted it. Do you not feel it? I know you do. Even as we stand here having this delightful conversation, the demon inside of you grows, desperate to be given life, dying to swallow you whole... so to speak."

"But I'm here to do a job. I'm on a mission."

"Oooo, really? Oh do tell!"

Fuck. Malachi was a stupid loud-mouthed twat! Lips and cock, lips and cock, the only two things I had to keep under control and I could not even do that.

"I shouldn't have said that. The point is, I'm not doing this for any personal gain and I'm certainly not doing this just for the hell of it."

"An interesting choice of words and really quite apt, old chap. But you see, the spirit world really is a funny old place and what you are doing is unnatural to them, perverted. Against God." He spat those last words as though they defiled his tongue. There seemed to be a lot of defiling going on in that room.

"Can I speak to them?" Suddenly I felt terrified. I was about to venture into a world I knew nothing about, a world I should know everything about. Was I ready? Did I really want to know the truth?

"Please, be my guest, I am sure they will be on their best behaviour while I am here."

My moment had arrived, but I was so nervous I farted. Thankfully, it was silent. I possessed my host's body, but its asshole was another matter.

"Who are you?"

"I was a baker."

"I was a butcher."

"I was a soldier."

"I was a Rabbi."

"I was a teacher."

"I was a factory worker." The list went on, normal people pulled out of their normal lives.

"I do not know who I was." My heart froze in my chest as I heard those words, sentiments that echoed my own and I looked at the man who spoke them. He was in his early twenties, plain looking and his uniform looked to be a few sizes too big for his slight frame.

"Ask them how they died." Melek winked at me encouragingly. God, he was cute.

I could not tear my gaze away from the nowhere man and

my lips quivered when I spoke. "How did you die?" My voice cracked as I felt an overwhelming wave of sadness crash over me. Many hands reached out and touched my body, touching every part of me. My mind exploded with violent images of pain and death. An old man clutched his chest in agony as his heart gave out, an entire group wiped out by starvation, a youngster raped and murdered by his Kapo, so much tragedy. My heart wept for them.

"I do not know how I died." His eyes were so sad, filled with emptiness and I could not help but wonder if I were looking into a mirror at myself.

"Do you remember anything, anything at all?"

"Nothing. I woke up in an empty container on a train. It was very dark and I was too afraid to move. Soldiers came, went, and I shouted at them, begged them to see me, to tell me what had happened but they could not see me, they could not hear me. I got so angry! No one would tell me what had happened." His eyes flashed yellow and I stepped back, my skin prickling in alarm.

"What did you do? Please, you must tell me..."

"I don't know how I did it, I didn't mean to. This man, he had the same uniform as me. He climbed into the container. He looked as though he was hiding and he was so frightened. I tried to talk to him, I got right down next to him, stuck my face in his. I screamed at him and he still couldn't hear or see me. And then suddenly I was in him, I was him. And Christ it felt good! But suddenly the doors to the container slid open and there were soldiers with riffles. I tried to explain to them, I put my hands out to warn them but it was too late, they fired, throwing me out of the body as it shattered. I must have passed out or something because the next thing I knew, the train came here. I saw the others, wandering so aimlessly amongst the living, so I followed them. They would not talk to me. And now I am here talking to you and we are the same."

For once, I was shocked into silence.

"Go now, all of you," commanded the devil and they shimmered from existence.

"You know what happened to him don't you, you know how he died."

"Yes."

"And you are not going to tell me are you?"

"No."

"So why show me this? What is the point?"

"Ah, the age-old question, asked by so many and yet the only question that ever goes unanswered."

"You know what I mean, you supercilious cunt." My language shocked me, but at the same time, it sent a delicious thrill through my body.

"I cannot interfere, Malachi, Father would be so cross. Who am I to disappoint Daddy?"

"And yet here you stand."

"I like you, Malachi, really I do. Rules are made to be... bent a little, shall we say. Are you telling me that you have learned nothing today?"

I sifted through my scrambled brain to process the pieces laid before me, little connections fusing together to form an idea. So many ghosts, but just one, one out of so many was like me. Why, what did that tell me? I could almost hear my head squeezing my brain, trying to get at the answer, trying to force it out of every wrinkle and crevice. Somewhere deep within my head a light, the faintest spark, flared into existence and I grabbed it, grateful for even that tiniest of insights.

"That I am not common."

"Oh I could have told you that, dear heart." He winked at me, the devil actually winked at me. It made my knees go weak. FFwarr.

"Don't be naughty, you know what I mean." I was flirting with the devil. Ha! "There were so many of them and just one like me, so that means I am different, special for some reason?"

"Go on."

I forced myself to think. What made me different from those who knew how they died? Why was I different, why was I special? Heart attacks, starvation, strangulation. They were horrible ways to die yes, but surely nothing out of the ordinary. Fuck. That was it — that was the point of difference. I was not special. It was the way that I died. The *way* I died was special.

"My death, my death was different, unusual. The way I died sets me apart from all the others, all the normal deaths."

Melek smiled so wide that the corners of his mouth almost touched his ears. It freaked me out a little. What I did not understand was *why* I was talking to him. What the fuck did Melek, the devil himself, want with me, why would *he* want to talk to me?

"What do you want, Melek? Why are you here, with me?"

"As I said, dear heart, I like you, you show such... promise. I love what you do with that body, by the way. Do keep up the good work."

"I won't be in it much longer."

"Oh what a shame, you wear it so well! And I particularly love that thing you do with the yellow eyes, it's so... alluring."

"Don't change the subject."

"I'm just saying, I think that demon hood will suit you and I look forward to welcoming you into the fold with open arms."

"Melek!"

"Take your fingers out of your ears, Malachi, and listen to

what I am trying to say to you." He spoke each word with laughter, his voice warm and charismatic, totally edible and damn it, I could not help it, I was attracted to him. I wanted him. I wanted him to bend me over there and then and stick it in me.

"I am trying, in my own inimitable way, to ask you the question."

"Fuck me pink and call me custard." He moved so close to me I could have licked his lips, his plump, juicy, cock sucking lips.

He leaned into me and whispered into my ear. "Custard." How he made that one word sound so god damned sexy I did not know. My skin shivered and my cheeks burned. If I reached out my hand, would that bulge in his trousers be hard? Did I dare?

"You want me to come with you?" He didn't move. He remained inches away from my face and his eyes so intense, so full of sincerity and I think that shocked me more than anything. He really did want me. I knew it, without doubt or hesitation. Melek wanted me.

"Yes. I want you, every bit of you."

And then he kissed me. His lips collided with mine, moving urgently against my flesh and they felt so moist. His tongue pushed its way between my lips, eager and explorative and his mouth moved with such expertise that it sent my body into the atmosphere. I felt like I was on fire and I could not stop myself, I didn't want to stop myself and I pushed back with my tongue, enjoying the wetness of his mouth inside of my own. To inhabit that human body was to live. To inhabit that body was to feel and right then, at that moment, all I could do was feel, feel him inside of me, feel his passion toward me hitting me like a storm breaching a pier and my world rocked with the impact of him against me.

My heart, my soldier's living heart, beat in my chest like a locomotive, pounding against my ribcage trying desperately to free itself. I felt it rising from within me, hot and fluid, pumping hard and filling me, my demon soaring through my veins, invading every nerve and fibre, burning through my eyes, taking possession of me. Raw unrestrained power surged through my body, for it no longer belonged to the soldier. I wanted to possess him, I desired him and I wanted to be in him. My hand, my clawed demon hand reached up and grabbed Melek by the hair and I pulled his head back, my tongue flicking over his neck, licking his plump lips and I could feel his blood pumping beneath their thin membrane of skin. It was all I could do to prevent myself from devouring him, because I wanted to put him in my mouth, all of him, to swallow him whole.

His head snapped up. "Well hello, sweetie." He grinned, his eyes burning, drilling deep into me.

What the fuck was I doing? What the fuck was happening to me? I was Malachi, I was not a demon, I was not the demon that he wanted me to be, and I would never be the demon he wanted me to be.

I pulled away, fighting against the monster clawing at my skin. I screamed in anger, my rage whipping around me like a tornado. My claws were tearing at the air, my feet pounding on the earth beneath me until finally, and with an effort that nearly tore me apart—I forced the demon away.

Melek was looking at me, his eyes simmering with desire and he was breathing heavily. It was nice to know I still had it.

"Impressive," he said breathlessly as he smoothed back his jet-black hair.

"It's the demon you want, isn't it, not me. You just want another soul to swell your ranks."

"Well, you made something swell, that's for sure."

"Does everything with you have to have an ulterior meaning?" I had come so close to giving in to that thing, to giving myself over to Melek in that moment of overwhelming passion. It made me jittery. And I was annoyed with myself because in reality, I wanted to say yes.

"Understand me, Malachi, I am no angel, I have a job to do, and believe me when I say I'm very good at it. Yes, I want you, yes I want you to complete your journey and become my demon. But listen to me now, I want you to be *my* demon, to become *my* right hand man, to stand at *my* side while I, *we* undertake our great work."

"And what work would that be?"

"Now, Malachi, dear heart..." he said as he circled me, his hand brushing against my clothes as he completed his lap, "but you can't expect me to give you everything in one go now, can you?"

"And yet you expect me to make a choice, based on what, trust? I do not think so."

His gentle laughter made me all gooey inside. How dare the bastard be so insufferably smooth?

"I lost my throne, Mal... I can call you Mal can't I? I lost my throne, and I want it back. I will have it back. Simples."

"So what are you going to do? Excuse me God, but I think you are sitting in my chair? Really?"

"Something like that."

"Yeah right."

"Mal, forget the details, I am asking you to be mine, to stand by my side. I am asking you the question and I hope with all my heart you can see it in yourself to say yes."

Damn his sincerity, Daniyyel wasn't that sincere. Daniyyel didn't shove his tongue down my throat. Daniyyel didn't offer me a throne.

So was that my lot, an afterlife in Heaven, or an eternity in Hell? Were those my choices? And what would that entail exactly?

Daniyyel might have asked me the question, but he did not give me a reason to say yes. What awaited me in Heaven? I had absolutely no idea because the angel gave me nothing, told me nothing. Did he assume that the offer, that the allure of going to Heaven was enough? Was that enough? Did the angel take it for granted that the mere act of offering a place in Heaven was enough to guarantee compliance? The angel presumed too much. His arrogance infuriated me.

Anger flared again, hot and fetid, it burned me.

But what about love, what about desire, passion and companionship, did any of that exist in Heaven?

And so the devil brought me his offer, a place in Hell, the burning pit of eternal damnation. But not just any place in Hell, oh no, but a place by his side, to take his hand, to be his with all the desire and passion that went with the job description, the chance to be a part of something, an opportunity for love.

Bugger the cost. I wanted it. My demon-self wanted it. But was I ready? Angel or demon, when I really wanted to be vampire.

"Can I take a rain check?" I thought I saw a flicker of disappointment flash across his piercing eyes and the smirk that creased his immaculately smooth face drooped slightly at the corners of his mouth.

"I am sorry to hear that, dear heart."

"I am not ready yet, too much unfinished business, you know, being a ghost and all. Do not think I do not appreciate it though. And do not give up on me," I added quickly.

"I have no intention of giving up on you. Unlike the offer from my opposite number, my invitation comes without strings and without an expiry date. You will see me again, and I will keep asking until you say yes. And if you should...

embrace your inner demon, well I will be there to take you by the hand."

He kissed me on the lips, a soft, almost whisper like sensation and I closed my eyes to enjoy the tingling sensation that coursed throughout my body. When I opened my eyes, he was gone.

I felt a stab of pain in my chest. It shocked me that his departure should induce such a reaction. I felt suddenly empty, hollow, alone. And maybe that feeling was telling me something. I had been so fixated on my life with Eli I had never stopped to think whether it was real, or if it was the only option available to me. Could I find love outside of Alte? Could I find a love reciprocated?

I needed to get out of that room. My world was spinning out of control and I felt fractured somehow, torn, both body and soul. The stifling heat from the furnace crushed me beneath its oppressive umbrella, its weight pressing down upon my shoulders, around my neck, suffocating my host and I needed to breathe.

The icy cold blast of air that hit my sweating skin felt mercifully refreshing and my host's lungs stung as I gulped in great gasps of chilled air. I felt dizzy, my vision blurred and it took me a moment to regain my equilibrium.

Running feet and excited voices shook me from my delirium. A hard, manly slap on my shoulder made me turn around and I looked up into the ugly but eager face of Stefan.

"Where you been, you daft fuck? Someone's tried to escape, come on quick before they clean up the mess, I don't want to miss this one."

I followed him, trying to run as butch as possible, without my arms swinging around like some demented windmill. There was a reason why gay men did not run.

A small crowd of soldiers had gathered at the base of the

perimeter fence and Stefan was eagerly pushing his way through to the front.

"He got half way up before they shot him," someone exclaimed excitedly.

"Ah, that's nothing, I saw one reach the top once, we didn't shoot him, wanted to see what the barbed wire would do to his skin. Tore him to shreds and he fell, split his head like a melon."

"No shit?"

"Honest, saw it with my own eyes."

As I reached the front of the crowd, their inane conversations faded from my ears. I heard nothing and saw nothing, only the crumpled body lying in the mud before me. It filled my eyes, the sight of it blocked out the sun, blocked out the light and I felt the gasp of horror escape from my lips before I could stop it.

"Ah it's not too bad," complained Stefan, "I thought his head would be split open at least."

I wanted to punch him, to turn him around and land my fist in his pathetic face. But all I could do was look down at that poor broken body of the boy from the furnace with his back arched unnaturally, blood already coagulating around a bullet wound to his side. His wide, dead eyes saw no more suffering. His mouth twisted into a faint smile of blessed release and every muscle, every detail whispered relief. I knew in my soul he was happy in death.

And then my heart broke.

Chapter Twenty: The Burning Dream, With Knobs On

There were so many of them, an endless sea of muscular figures, but I could not see their faces. Every time I tried to look, their features blurred. As I moved through the throng of hard pectorals, the bodies parted with a whisper of cloth and urgent voices, two words intoned with a vitality that undulated through the masses as they split apart before me into two groups.

"It's him."

Those two words moved outward exponentially like the ripples on the surface of a pond, their cadence rising with an almost hypnotic intensity until the air was alive with their resonance. The sound overlapped, bounced back, hitting me with both waves of accusation and admiration, a confusing cacophony of directed thought that left me mystified as to their intention.

Empathy pulsed from the one side while revulsion battered me from the other. Love and hate embodied in beauty. I had to concentrate and focus all my attention on the path ahead to prevent the disparity of emotions from drowning me.

What had I done?

Something blocked my path, a hunched, cowering form that lay directly ahead, arms and legs tucked protectively beneath his body. My eyes saw but my brain refused to believe.

I did not want to see. I could not bear to see. My eyes shed bitter tears in agony.

But I did see. That magnificent muscular frame, those piercing green eyes that looked up at me with such terror, such pleading and those full lips so cruelly cracked and bleeding, lips I had so longed to kiss. I reached out to him, my rescued enigmatic stranger, to Ethan.

Our fingers reached out across the short distance, desperate to touch, desperate for solace and comfort. The very tips of our index fingers touched, a spark passing between them and my arms filled with a warmth that flooded my body, filling my head with a joy both unexpected and shocking.

That simple display of intimacy acted as a signal that saw the two opposing armies shifting on either side of me. Moving in perfect unison and synchronicity, they raised their swords above their heads, the flaming lengths of polished metal blazing white hot and hissing.

Suddenly my world became a torture of blood and clashing metal. Thick rivulets of red rained down upon me, filling my vision with gore, offending my sanity with dismembered limbs. Everything turned crimson. War raged, fierce and uncompromising, brutal. I stood in the middle of two opposing armies drenched in their blood.

The ground beneath me shook and the floor heaved, threatening to topple me with every thunderous undulation. He was coming. The one who I had disappointed was coming. And boy was He pissed off.

Disappointment, I could almost smell it, thick and cloying. Heavy, crushing waves of bitter disappointment mixed with a dose of fierce anger. My stomach churned as the emotions hit me, fear rising with the bile in my throat, the terror and the guilt suffocating. My bowels turned to liquid, pouring down my quivering legs.

The guilt was so heavy I could barely carry the weight of it.

"You did this!" The army bellowed their accusation in perfect unity.

I needed to run, to wrap my shame around me and hide, flee from the wrath of He who felt so betrayed.

He was very close. I could feel his shadow looming over me. I could feel the weight of his condemning presence waiting to bring down his mighty wrath upon me without mercy. I cowered, my shame so obvious, I reeked of it, it poured from me in thick rivulets of despair, and I knew there was nowhere to hide, nowhere to hide from Him.

But why did I feel guilty? I had done nothing wrong. I had done fuck-all to be ashamed of, so why did I feel so ashamed? I was proud of what I was, love was a thing to be cherished, to be celebrated, in all its forms and manifestations and I was not about to bow down and beg for forgiveness for something I could not help.

My fear changed to anger, to rebellious rage and I felt liberated, freed at last from the manacles of conformity, no longer willing to hide what I was. I did not choose to be that way – I was born that way. I felt the words swelling in my chest, building in my throat as that terrible shadow grew closer. I stopped running and I turned around to stare into His terrible face. I give the words freedom and they exploded from my lips.

"It's not my fault! You made me this way!"

The thrill of defiance was short lived as a bellow of rage catapulted me into infinity and the scream that deafened my ears was my own.

Falling. Falling.

My skin split across my tumbling body, blood pouring from the wounds to harden into a thick scorched crust. My eyes exploded and my lips curled back blackened from my glowing skull, peeling away from my head, melting into the thick carapace that consumed my body. I was a comet, my tail the debris of my existence. I was the sun, my flesh burning white hot.

Plummeting. The space around me erupted in white-hot flame. A series of sonic booms ripped through my body and the ground loomed up to caress my burning magnificence in a bone-shattering embrace. The pain went beyond my understanding, beyond my ability to endure and yet I still felt it, but I had no tongue or lips with which to scream and all I could do was pray that my torture would soon be over.

The impact cracked the hard crust encasing my body. It shattered and split in a sticky ashen mosaic, pulling chunks of flesh *from my hot, shattered bones. I lay in a crater of my own obliteration.*

Just as I thought the pain could get no worse, my body began to heal. Bones started to move beneath my devastated carcass, moving through torn and savaged flesh with a life of their own, pulling themselves back together. Muscle, sinew, nerve endings, all grew back with frightening and painful speed, pulling my devastated form from the ashes of destruction. I could feel my tongue growing inside my mouth, lips creeping across my ravaged face. My eyes started to reform. Fluid pumped into the sockets, filling the gelatinous orbs and my newly formed mouth cried out in agony.

Suddenly everything was blinding white light. With a sound like crinkling paper, something unfurled against my forming eyeballs then my eyelids blinked, once, twice. Then all was clear.

I stared up into a beautiful cobalt blue sky. Insubstantial clouds of white fluffy vapours whispered across the expanse above, oblivious to my fall, and I felt jealous of their freedom, of their innocence. As I sat up, the ash fell from my naked body, then something extraordinary happened. My chest filled with air both clean and pure, and I felt my lungs expand, filling the cavity behind my ribs.

I was breathing. I was alive.

The colours that assaulted my senses were almost too vivid for me to comprehend, and it took a moment for my new eyes to become accustomed to the lusciousness that surrounded me. There were trees and bushes, heavy with plump, lush green leaves, their boughs weighed down with huge waxen flowers whose stamens glistened with dew. So many colours boldly painted across a tapestry of green, so many shapes. The beauty of it overwhelmed me.

A flicker, so fast, accompanied by a thrumming sound and a flash of blue, materialised as if from nowhere above a huge yellow bloom. The hummingbird hovered effortlessly above the throat of the huge flower, its wings beating so fast as to be invisible and gently, it inserted its long beak into the flower to drink the life giving nectar that dwelt within.

Something moved — a thick undulating thing that glistened sickly through the trees. Its body was as thick as a grown man's leg, its face a pointed snout of pure malignancy with black beady eyes that radiated pure evil. Suddenly the head of the serpent streaked out of the bush and its huge jaws snapped down, plucking the bird straight out of the air. The serpent looked at me. A sly smirk crept across its cruel mouth.

With a single gulp, the snake swallowed its victim, the bird moving down the length of its immense undulating stomach. A forked tongue flickered in and out of its mouth toward me, tasting the air, tasting my fear and I wanted nothing more than to escape its cold stare, to block the foul thing from my mind.

More movement, pushing through the trees either side of the serpent, filled me with a sense of overwhelming dread. Two figures emerged flanking the serpent, male and female with impossibly long limbs, their faces wrong somehow, inhuman, unfinished. The Mother and Father's cold eyes fell upon me and I shuddered under the weight of their hatred.

The Father raised his hands to stroke the serpent. Long spidery fingers wrapped around its girth, sliding up and down, the movement obscene, escalating in speed and intensity as the serpent shuddered with pleasure. The Mother oozed around to face it, her movements slinky and seductive. She bent down, her lips caressing those of the serpent, their tongues darting in and out of each other's wet mouths, tasting each other.

The bile rose in my throat, but I dared not open my mouth for fear of the scream building at the back of my throat.

The Father's hands moved faster, urgent, his face alive with ecstasy. The snake closed its eyes and opened its mouth. The Mother wrapped her lips around the snakes head as it ejaculated into her mouth, a mixture of blood and feathers spurting down her throat and across her face.

My mouth opened wide as the vomit shot past my lips and my scream burst from my throat in undiluted waves of terror.

Suddenly the ground beneath me lurched. The earth cracked and rumbled and I was falling, the earth devouring me in darkness.

Blackness enveloped me as I tumbled helplessly through the ground. I travelled down a tube, the walls black and glassy smooth, reflecting my somersaulting nakedness in a wildly spinning collage of images until I emerged into a vast cathedral sized space. Black stalactites flashed past in a blur and light flickered wildly from below, yellow and red, an immense fiery pit burning in an endless chasm. I plummeted toward those flames powerless to stop my trajectory, falling toward those consuming tongues of red, my scream devoured by darkness.

A plateau of rock rose out of the flames below and I landed with a thud upon its glassy surface. The palms of my hands lay flat against the stone and yet, despite the searing maelstrom that surrounded me, the stone remained cool to the touch. My naked skin flinched at the sight of the flames that leaped hungrily toward it and yet I felt no heat.

Huge curtains of liquid flame erupted from the depths, flaming fingers reaching into the blackness above in a pyrotechnic ballet of light. White-hot tendrils licked the stalactite studded ceiling causing their sharp crystalline tips to glow white then red, the effect rippling across the high ceiling in waves of sparkling incandescence. To find such mesmerising beauty in the asshole of the world blew my mind. Fire terrified me, but in that cathedral of flame, it seemed so alive and it was showing off, treating me to a glittering show, a cascade of light and colour to rival the heavens themselves.

Something moved in the burning lake beneath me. The surface of liquid fire heaved and broiled as though something massive moved through its depths and a tide of flame, white hot and molten, splashed outward from the wake. Suddenly something huge erupted through the inferno, sending comets of burning debris flying into the air. An arm, so huge and muscular it dwarfed me. My eyes refused to see what was in front of me, the enormity of it towering above me like a skyscraper of raw flesh and muscle. I could see muscle and sinew moving beneath its virtually transparent skin as the gigantic hand clenched and unclenched with startling power. A thick intricate network of pulsing black veins sat on the surface of the arm, wriggling and squirming as it pumped thick black viscous liquid through its walls.

A sound akin to twisting metal roared from the fiery lake as the rest of the body began to heave itself to the surface. More transparent skin and musculature assaulted my eyes, sinew and tendons undulating beneath a shower of liquid fire as the colossus surfaced. I could see its heart beating inside its chest, a heart the size of a horse, beating and trembling inside a complex structure of black veins and tendons.

I had to look up. I had to look into the face of that monstrous being, even though I didn't want to look, even though every fibre of my being warned me not to look, because I knew that if I did, I would never be the same again. But I had to see, my eyes lifted, my eyes saw and my heart shuddered.

My eyes took in the huge head with its thick plump lips, lips made of muscle and sinew beneath transparent flesh. The tendons tugged at the muscles, pulling them into a grimace that was somehow camp and yet terrifying at the same time. A tongue slithered inside the head – I could see it writhing within the mouth cavity, brushing across needle sharp teeth.

And those eyes, huge yellow orbs set within lidless sockets. Yellow as the sun, reflecting every conceivable colour in a rainbow of pure malignance, they burned with hatred. I could feel their gaze tearing through me, devouring me.

But I knew that face. How could I not? That smile was instantly recognisable to me. It was Malachi.

Words hissed though his lips, his breath hot and foul against my flesh, a sound both thick and sibilant.

"Is it fair do you think? Did I not give you enough?"

Another sound echoed through the cavern. Roar upon devastating roar, overlapping and undulating, ricocheting and rebounding. It made my skin shiver. The ground shook and heaved at the sound of approaching footsteps and Malachi looked ecstatic, a groan of orgasmic pleasure escaping from his lips as the flaming sea around him surged at the approach of something massive.

A shadow swept across my pinnacle of rock as something moved around from behind me. I kept my eyes down, afraid to look up, but I could see immense legs, inhuman legs, legs covered in a thick matting of coarse grey hair. An arm, also thickly matted and ending in a fist of cruel claws, swung past me so close I could not help but recoil, falling onto my back. Panic forced me to reach backward to prevent myself from plummeting into the boiling flames, and in that brief uncontrolled moment, my eyes flickered upward.

I saw a pair of horns, massive twisted spears of bone that protruded from a head with a face too terrible to behold. The snout, the teeth, the monstrous yellow eyes that blazed with such intent, such intelligence, the tongue, forked and glistening, the whole forming an image from the realm of nightmares.

The Beast embraced Malachi, pulling him into his arms, and their mouths clashed fiercely, tongues exploring, his hands caressing his flesh with such tenderness, every touch imbued with intense feeling and love, an act so intimate I felt myself blush. Suddenly the Beast turned Malachi around, a massive clawed hand pushing his head down so that his backside thrust against his groin. The Beast pushed into him.

Malachi's head turned and smiled at me.

"Have you met my new boyfriend?"

The sound that filled the cavern and obliterated all was the sound of my screaming.

Chapter Twenty-one: Dead Camp Five

As related by Eli

Shouting forced me from my nightmare with a start. The sound frightened me, the terror of my dream still so vivid, and it made me jump, my body turning icy cold with shock. I felt disorientated, dizzy and for a moment, I did not know if the shouting was my own or if the darkness that met my startled eyes belonged to the haunting remains of my dreamscape.

A sharp slap across my face brought reality crashing back. My eyes cut through the gloom to see the Kapo leering over me with saliva and half-eaten food hanging from the corner of his mouth.

I was going to stick his cock so far up his own ass he would be able to suck himself off.

"Move, now, you fucking cock sniping bastards. Down to the loading bays, we have guests to meet."

Guests, that meant *they* were arriving. My past had caught up with my present to fuck me up the shitter, again. I thought to be gone from that hellhole by the time they arrived. I thought to avoid the sight of their ugly faces, to escape the feel of their impenetrable evil engulfing my life, but too late. The Mother, The Father and me, together once more, happy fucking days.

The inevitability of it crushed me. My entire sorry existence was building up to that one moment when I would have to stand my ground and face them, those fucking bastards who ruined my life. London was round one. The bell was ringing and round two was about to start.

Rain poured down as we marched in single file to the train depot, heavy, ice-cold globules falling from a grey sky to soak grey, listless people, the churning mud beneath our feet adding to the overwhelming misery that gripped our hearts.

So many lost souls, so much suffering, so much despondency in a sea of people betrayed. I felt their loss of hope and I felt their loss of dignity. I had never been a part of humanity, never felt like one of them. I was vampire, immortal, Menarche, and yet I had always yearned to be a part of them, to feel like them, to live like them. And there I was, my wish fulfilled, as close to the human race as I had ever been, and I suffered with them. I felt their despair.

To be human was to suffer. To be human was to be humiliated and beaten. To be human was to be both oppressor and oppressed.

As the crowd coalesced into two groups either side of the gates, my head spun. Humanity was getting to me, their pain infecting me, making me sick, making me weak. Pain stabbed through my stomach, my vision rippled and I thought for one terrible moment I would pass out.

My beautiful hands withered before my eyes as black veins spread out across my flesh, pulsing and throbbing with hunger. I had to control my thirst before my vampire won out.

"You don't look too good." I had not noticed the Nazi troops before us, forming a perfectly straight path down the centre of the prisoners. Malachi stood in front of me whispering discreetly over his shoulder.

"I'm hungry, I haven't fed in days." The thought of sucking on a Nazi made me feel sick and the thought of feeding off a prisoner disgusted me.

Had that camp *changed* me that much? It was not so long ago that those same soldiers were fucking me in the woods, and I never had a second thought about snacking on one.

Was that guilt crippling me, or humanity?

"You have to, if you don't get the party started down here, how am I to get Isaiah out?"

"Have you found him?"

"He's definitely in the castle but I can't get to him. SS only. He will be coming to meet them from the train."

"Don't you worry about me — you just do your bit."

"You must feed."

"I can't."

"You must."

The whistle of a train and the tell-tale plumes of white smoke billowing above the tree line signalled the arrival of monsters.

Silence fell over Welwelsburg Castle. The atmosphere darkened, charged with anticipation and dread, radiating pinpricks of fear that danced across the crowd as all eyes followed the rapidly approaching smoke.

Huge and gleaming, the locomotive chugged onto the platform with its arms turning doom-laden wheels that screeched their underlying horror as unseen hands threw the brakes home. Metal on metal, grinding the monster to an inexorable end as steam erupted with a violent hiss from around its black carcass. With a final, defiant shudder, the locomotive came to a squealing halt, its death throes echoing into the surrounding trees.

It was no ordinary train. The locomotive resembled a killer whale, glistening black with a huge swastika blazed proudly across its side, emanating a thick penetrating evil that made the air itself tremble with shame. It pulled three long torpedo shaped carriages, with thick velvet drapes adorning their sparkling windows, piercing the black carriages with flashes of emerald-green pile and gold fringing.

Behind the art deco torpedoes sat a dozen freight carts, huge faceless carriages that brought death to Welwelsburg Castle, an unspeakable creeping terror that the Nazis intended to rain down from the skies on an unsuspecting and helpless population. Trains full of evil in wooden boxes.

The welcoming committee, headed by the Blockfürher, oozed nervously toward the front carriage, and it amused me to see the greasy fat fucker cringe as the doors opened, spilling forth a gaggle of SS troops who stood to attention on the platform, their monstrous uniforms a symbol of hatred and brutality.

I wanted to sink my teeth into their fragile necks and drink deep, and it was all I could do to resist the temptation to help myself to the buffet cart.

Suddenly, in a flurry of upheld arms, a series of figures descended onto the platform. They emerged as a flock of black ravens, glistening and shiny in their black leather caps and trench coats, slick as oil and just as slippery, but I did not recognise their faces. A new generation of Vril, fresh blood for an organisation that grew like a cancerous growth in the middle of mankind's body, devouring it with murderous intent and calculating efficiency. But the Vril themselves remained human, fanatics ensconced within a powerful supernatural cult, pawns to their masters, and it was their masters that worried me, the Thule.

With the grovelling and handshaking over, two officers escorted the black clad Vril members down the aisle, and I felt the crowd around me hold their breaths in collective fear. But the terrified faces of humans meant nothing to the Vril — until, that was, they stood before me.

The black pariahs stopped abruptly. A short wiry man with round glasses and a weasel face scanned the crowd before him, his black full-length coat billowing outward in the wind like wings as he scanned the crowd with blazing, unearthly eyes that moved from face to face with cold purpose. Ice-cold fingers of fear clawed at my spine. Could he see me? Could he sense me somehow?

And then, out of the corner of my eye, I saw it. Something hunched on his shoulder, a lump that squirmed wetly beneath his clothes. If I looked directly at his face the apparition vanished, but if I turned my head slightly I could see it, just visible at the edge of my perception.

The flash of a grey tentacle creeping across the flesh of his neck, the flicker of a yellow eye, piercing and vibrant with cruel intelligence, and I realised with mounting dismay I had seen that thing before, the demon offspring of the Mother, Quellor Demons.

Isaiah had spoken of such things in his diary, shapeless lumps of horror disgorged from the Mothers loins. He saw one placed onto Hitler's back and Ethan saw one on the back of a feral vampire in Berlin.

I had once killed a Quellor Demon with my bare hands. I pulled it apart tentacle by flaying tentacle. But Quellor Demons were adaptive creatures and symbiotic by nature — they required a host to attain their full potential, to awaken their latent supernatural power. Once bound to a host, they joined with the life force of that creature, enhancing both the host's strength and their own, making them virtually indestructible to all mortal weapons. The hosts became slaves to the Mother, controlled through the evil offspring latched onto their shoulders.

To bind them to humans was bad enough — it would create a race of super humans subservient to the Mother, cunning, intelligent, almost immortal. But to bind them to feral vampires, creatures already immortal, to give them intelligence, to give them purpose and direction. An army of such monsters could wipe mankind from the face of the earth.

I shrank back into the crowd in a vain attempt to become invisible, but the Vril raised his arm and swept it across our section of prisoners. Two words spat from between his tight lips.

"Clean them." They continued on their way, a flock of black vultures.

Hunger made me sloppy. I should not have stood at the front. I could not think straight—everywhere my eyes turned, I saw them, the Vril, my enemy, the enemy of all things living. Veins pulsed at the corners of my eyes and I thought I would collapse as my head reeled at the sight of them. The Vril, the Quellor Demons on their backs, the audacity of their dreams and the horror it would inflict upon a defenceless world, and I felt lost, small. It was hopeless. They had arrived, and I was impotent with fear and hunger.

Then *they* came out of the train. Tall sub-human creatures, The Mother and The Father, the Original Menarche, faces devoid of character, limbs long and gangly with huge round eyes that shone with malevolence. Everything about them was alien, and as they crawled from the interior of the train I could feel everybody, the Blockfürher included, recoil from their presence. I already knew them to be Menarche, but to the eyes of others, they were the unknown, different, inhuman, and the crowd watching their awkward movements, felt it, and shrank away from their horror.

Each wore their own unique version of the SS uniform. He wore a black gloss suit, so tight it clung to him like a second skin. A black leather cape rippled across his shoulders, the material heavy and unyielding, giving the impression of an insect's carapace, and atop his oversized head sat a wide brimmed black fedora. She wore a black glossy dress that clung to every curve and womanly crevice, with a skirt so short I could see what she ate for breakfast. The bodice, tight and shaped like an hourglass, cupped her pale breasts, and she too wore a matching cape of leather that fell over her shoulders and down her arms.

The Father extended a long hand toward the Blockfürher, who could barely conceal a shudder at his touch. The Father's fingers wrapped around the Blockfürher's hand completely, and the terror on his face was palpable, but when the fingers uncurled, moving individually from around his trembling hand, he looked faint. Then the Mother stepped forward and bent down to brush his cheek with her lips, her tongue flicking out to lick a bead of perspiration that tumbled from his sweating brow, savouring the taste of his fear as it filled her mouth. She smiled with smug satisfaction.

I knew how satisfying the taste of fear could be.

The Blockfürher wiped the sweat off his palms, then used a dirty handkerchief to mop his soaking face before indicating with an awkward bow for the Thule to follow him. The two Menarche scuttled behind the Blockfürher, their eyes devouring each other, oblivious to the terrified audience. He held his long hands before him, one hand draped across the other, long fingers dangling beneath his wrists, and the image that Isaiah painted of a praying mantis swam vividly into my mind. She sashayed from side to side, one long hand resting on his shoulder, nail-less fingers playing absentmindedly with the lapel of his suit. Their gazes never left each other.

I shrank further into the crowd behind, terrified they would see me, or smell me. I had killed their son, their one true son, Morbius. They would rip the crowd limb from limb to get at me.

An old man appearing from the direction of the castle puffed to a halt in front of the Thule. His old wrinkled eyes regarded the two figures with disgust, and I could not help but admire his bald-faced courage. She reached out a hand and brushed his face gently, but he pushed it away and continued toward the train.

I liked him instantly.

He was a large man with a heavy tweed raincoat that had obviously seen better days. He wore a black skullcap and wiry glasses, badly repaired with brown packing tape, perched on his fat nose. Clutched protectively to his chest was a large worn carpetbag. He seemed very impatient, hopping from one foot to the next while glaring at something inside the train, eager for it to emerge.

I knew who it was the moment he stood up to the Thule. It was Isaiah.

He waited with annoyance at the bottom of the stairs as two uniformed officers carried out, with some difficulty, a huge wooden chest. He reached out with tentative fingers and brushed its surface gently, a look of reverence creasing his old face. With a snap of his fingers, he scurried away, the officers following with their heavy load, but he glanced back occasionally, his gaze reluctant to leave the chest.

As he passed, I got a good look at his face. Time and circumstance had not been kind to Isaiah Silberman. He had seen great evil, fought great evil, and his face betrayed that terrible knowledge. He knew what it was that lurked in the darkness. That face had witnessed the death of his wife—his round wild eyes had seen her resurrected, and his memories carried the vision of his son destroying the monster his wife had become. He was a man caught between two worlds, a victim of terrible circumstance.

He was a man who tried to help another and ended up losing everything.

Isaiah was me and I was Isaiah.

My vampire eyes could see beyond the scars, beyond the

pain and anguish, the torment that distorted his face. I could
see the handsome man he once was, the boy who discovered
the existence of monsters and fell in love with a pretty young
volunteer in a cookhouse. But he wore his past and his
present so heavily it crushed his soul beneath a black cloud,
a cloud he could not escape, that would not allow him to
escape—the man he once aspired to be gone, threatened by
all-consuming evil wearing shiny black leather.

That was Isaiah Nathan Silberman.

Could I abandon those innocents trapped within that
death camp? Could I fly Isaiah to safety? It crossed my
mind. If I scooped him up in my arms and flew away, would
it be over?

No. It would never be over, for either of us.

A loud mechanical groan halted all thoughts of escape as,
to my utter astonishment, the entire side of the third carriage
started to open. The façade of the carriage moved on a hinge
concealed at its base, screeching open in a cloud of white
steam until, with a loud metallic clang, it dropped onto the
concrete platform, revealing an undulating wall of dense
vapour. A jet of steam erupted from within, hissing outward
with incredible force, multiple ejaculations of writhing mist
that drifted to the floor to swirl around our feet. Then silence
fell upon Welwelsburg, as impenetrable as the misty wall
before us.

Ticking, it drifted through the smoke, a rhythmic,
clockwork beat. And then the wall of smoke bulged
outward.

The mechanical monolith pushed its way out of the
dissipating cloud and moved down the ramp onto the
platform, a machine of unbelievable complexity at whose
heart lay embedded a huge block of ice. Jets of steam issued
from tubes and coils amid wheels and cogs that ticked and
whirred. As it drew nearer, I could see a black shape encased

within the ice, like an insect trapped in amber, obscured by layer upon layer of crystals, a vaguely humanoid form upon which the tubes and wires converged.

My skin erupted with goose flesh and every hair on my body stood on end. I felt drawn toward it, my eyes magnetised to the thing at its heart as though it were calling to me, as though it wanted me, demanded me. I pushed my way through the crowd toward the front, not caring who saw me, indifferent to the danger — all that mattered was the ice. I had to get inside it. I had to see the thing inside.

"Don't be so fucking stupid, Eli, get back." Malachi pushed me back sharply. I had forgotten he was there, but I could barely hear his words — they meant nothing to me. All that mattered was that thing, frozen, suspended, waiting to be set free, calling me to set it free.

His fist collided with my face with a violent crack, sending me sprawling into the mud. I looked at him through shocked eyes as he bent over my prostrate form, his face contorted into an ugly sneer. He really was acting the part.

"Get back in line, you filthy bastard!" He followed his punch with a sly wink. I nodded, half-dazed, grateful for his timely intervention. I scrabbled to my feet and fell back into line, just in time to see the clockwork monstrosity pass.

But the procession wasn't over as a group of six soldiers, carrying a stretcher between them, marched past with perfect military precision, arms swinging in long deliberate arches, legs lifted in long stiff strides while the load carried between them remained level and steady. A body lay upon the stretcher, hidden beneath a shroud of emerald-green brocade and resting on top of that sat a huge golden cauldron, heavily embellished with intricate scrolls and figures that wound their curlicue forms around its glittering circumference. The gold seemed to capture every speck of available light in its lustrous surface, glowing like a miniature sun of exquisite craftsmanship and beauty.

Suddenly I felt sick. Bile filled my throat and stung my lips. I clutched my stomach as wave upon wave of nauseating pain tore through my bowels. I could barely stop myself from shouting. My eyes fixed on the shape beneath the shroud, its shrivelled outline inexplicably fascinating to me—there was something so familiar about it, not physically, not visually, but a smell, the faintest of odours, a feeling. I wanted nothing more than to rip that shroud from the stretcher, to gaze upon the twisted shape, to see with my own eyes what lay concealed beneath, to recognise it, to put a name to the outline that tortured me so much. But the pain kept me rooted to the spot and I could not move. The thing was taunting me. It wanted me to know, it wanted me to see it. But the pain, pain that shredded me from the inside.

Arms pushed me, mindless figures shoving me forward. I had not even noticed that the stretcher was gone. Dazed and confused, I watched my fellow prisoners move down to the platform, shuffling aimlessly toward the cargo carriers. I felt lost, I felt bereaved, filled with nothing but unending horror, unending pain.

"Move! Bring the boxes to the enclosure."

Sanity returned with merciful clarity and I stumbled forward with the crowd toward the freights where soldiers held us at gunpoint. Every nerve in my body yelled at me to run, to flee that place and the horrors about to unfold, and every gaunt face before those cargo freights betrayed the same desperate emotion. The smell of fear and apprehension that leeched from my fellow inmates filled my nostrils. It was intoxicating to me, fuelling my hunger, demanding my undivided attention, demanding I rip open a throat and drink. The smell of fear always did that to me—it was like an Hors d'oeuvre, the promise of a feast yet to come. Mal was right, I needed to feed and soon, for everyone's sake.

The doors of the containers slid open with a shriek, and the stench that erupted from the interior made me gag. The thick smell of vomit and faeces mixed with the exhilarating scent of metallic blood and decay to assault my senses, and I swayed as I inhaled. I could almost taste the blood on the air, the heady coppery tang thick upon my tongue. I had to concentrate to stop my vampire manifesting, but all the same, I could feel the prick of my fangs piercing my bottom lip, drawing blood. I licked my lips, the taste of my own blood filling my mouth, teasing me. I swallowed, hard, forcing it back, willing myself forward into the filthy interior while the others held back, terrified. But the blood was calling to me.

I stood on the brink of darkness. I knew nothing but the smell of blood. My hands moved by themselves, reaching for the edge of the opening, feeling the wood beneath my clawed fingers, pulling me upward toward the blood, dragging me into madness.

I felt wild with hunger, my desperate thirst driving me insane.

I breathed deep, the irresistible taste of blood hitting the back of my throat, tickling my tongue with exquisite taste. The minute particles of blood coating my taste buds snapped my eyes into sharp focus and suddenly I could see them all around me, a forest of boxes, each with a large black swastika burned onto their surfaces. There must have been at least two dozen of them—two dozen of them, just in that one container. I placed my hand against the nearest box, palm flat against its rough pine surface, trying to sense what was inside, to feel the creature I knew to be sleeping within the safety of its dark interior.

I pressed my ear against the wood. The darkness around me seemed to intensify, blackness infringing the edges of my vision as I concentrated, listening for the slightest movement, the faintest sound, but only silence filled the void.

Something slithered against the sawdust-covered floor off to my right, and for a moment I was blind with fright. Cold ripples of fear cascaded down my body in rivers of undiluted panic.

Something black and glistening slithered between two boxes. Terror hissed between my lips with an involuntary squeal. The lack of food had weakened my resolve, made me jumpy—at least that was my excuse. With a supreme effort of will, I forced my legs to propel me forward cautiously through the forest of boxes, toward the far wall of the interior and that black crawling thing.

Thud! Slap! Something collided with the back wall and slid to the floor.

The smell of fear filled my nostrils. Whatever was lurking at the rear of the carriage was human.

Without thought, without care, I rushed forward, dire need and desperation propelling me on, and I found the SS soldier slumped against the wall, dying, with barely a breath left in his collapsing lungs. I swooped down on him, tilting his head to the side to reveal his throat, my fangs fully extended and my hands monstrous talons against his skin.

Two puncture marks winked back at me. Someone had bled him already, almost to the point of death, but maybe he had a little left in his collapsing veins, just enough blood to stave off my terrible hunger. I bore down on him, his eyes already beginning to glaze over with death, and I sank my teeth into the wounds so conveniently provided.

I was a hypocrite, a monster feeding on a monster.

I barely had time to gulp down two mouthfuls before his heart stopped beating. There was nothing left, just a dry dead corpse already cold in my hands, and I withdrew from his throat roughly, my teeth ripping his dead flesh apart in frustration. I savoured every last drop, licking it greedily from my lips and my teeth. I pulled my vampire back, feeling my hunger subside, relieved at the respite offered by so very little.

The soldier's life crept painfully through my veins, pulsing through my temples, the life of a sadist, a life wasted to cruelty, a life given in duty.

Why were my eyes moistening, why such guilt? He was dying anyway — nothing could have saved him. I didn't kill him. It was not my fault. His death did not belong to me. I just took what I needed, just enough to keep me going — his death would help to free the prisoners, prisoners condemned by the likes of him.

He deserved to die.

I kept telling myself that, over and over in my head. But it offered no comfort.

The sharp crack of rifle fire startled me and a chunk of wood exploded above my head. I spun around to see a figure outlined in the bright rectangle of the doors.

"Stop fucking about in there! Start bringing out the boxes... you... get in there and help him!"

Another body heaved itself into the interior. He gazed around terrified, his eyes wide with undisguised dread as he saw the boxes.

"Don't be afraid." I tried to sound comforting, but my words felt and sounded hollow. "They can't harm you."

"Death, there's death in those boxes." The poor fool trembled violently, pole-axed with fear.

"Death will take the form of a bullet if you don't help me move these boxes, now come on."

I grabbed the nearest box, tipping it onto its side toward the man who caught it reluctantly.

Something thudded inside the box. A scream of absolute terror burst from my comrade, who dropped the box, and the heavy wooden crate collided with the floor with a resounding bang. He backed away whimpering. I saw him outlined in the light of the door, hands raised to the sky in prayer, and his words made me feel sick. My vision exploded with red dots. My god, he was such a believer, so much faith, and his faith was burning me.

I held out my hands toward him, desperate for him to stop, pleading for him to be quiet, and I staggered forward but I was falling, the burning dream searing through my head, crippling me.

A sharp crack zinged through the interior. Then there was silence. For a moment, I saw the figure of the prisoner frozen in a rectangle of light, his hands still outstretched toward the heavens, but even in silhouette, I could see half his head was missing. His body fell backward and was gone.

Shock, pain, fear, disgust, helplessness, all emotions alien to my system, but before I could gather myself, before I could pull myself together, another figure was thrust into the carriage and came toward me.

"Help me, my friend," he whispered, "they are boxes, just boxes, let us move them, and quickly." I could have kissed him for his kindness.

We picked up the fallen box and heaved it toward the light, pushing it out toward expectant hands. Death, gift wrapped in wood. One box after another, lifted out into the light. What would happen if just one of those boxes were to crash to the floor and expose the deadly contents to the burning fingers of God?

I had no doubt there would be no one left to tell the tale. Slaughter would meet such carelessness, with the purification of the bullet.

We undertook the task in silence and with grim determination. Not a whisper passed between tight lips. The eyes said it all. The legend of the boxes had obviously spread across Germany like the Angel of Death, touching some and passing over others, and no amount of blood-smeared crosses could save you. How many towns had they visited? How many lives left decimated by their touch?

By the time we had finished emptying the three freights, it was getting dark. The sun was setting early over Welwelsburg Castle, too ashamed to illuminate the place any longer, ducking down behind the surrounding mountaintops with shame. Angry clouds roiled over our heads threatening to release their fury with bitter efficiency, a damning rage of hail and thunder to cut through our thin clothes in a deluge of misery. Half a dozen souls had perished already, collapsing to the floor, half frozen and exhausted, dying where they fell. We were forced to work around them at gunpoint, their bodies crushed underfoot, obscured by mud, and sometimes we could not help but step on them. It sickened me to my core. I would never forget the sound of bone snapping underfoot.

Over a hundred boxes filled the field in neat orderly rows, like dominoes. If I pushed one over, would they tumble? But with daylight rapidly evaporating, I could not help but wonder what would happen when darkness touched the field of wooden coffins? Would they disgorge their hungry contents on the camp? Would they run loose, to feed as they chose, or would the lumpy forms on their backs control them? Whatever was going to happen, it would happen soon, because I felt the darkness approaching and it made my blood tingle. Although I could walk by day, the night held a certain fascination for me. It called to me, excited me, empowered me. I was vampire, after all.

The answer arrived on the back of a flatbed truck. To my dismay, a huge mound of rope and wooden crucifixes filled the truck, crucifixes two feet tall. Having carried the damn coffins, they now expected us to bind them, wrapping the ropes around each box with a crucifix caught between the box and the rope, locking the beasts within.

I had to look away. If I looked at one—and god help me if I touched one—it would cripple me with blinding pain, the disapproving hand of God stabbing me in the face, and no amount of artifice would hide my true nature. Even without looking, I could *feel* them, their proximity making my skin crawl, making me nauseous, poisoning me with their piety.

A gentle hand touched my shoulder and a voice, kind and sympathetic, whispered into my ear.

"You don't have to touch them. Let me help you." I looked up, cold beads of sweat already forming on my furrowed brow, straight into the face of a young man, the same young man who had shaved my head upon my arrival. He looked at me without fear, without incrimination, just kindness and an understanding that moved me. He had cut me that day, his sheers slicing into my skin, and he had seen me heal, the wound knitting together right before his eyes. He had felt the coldness of my touch, seen the pallor of my skin. He had called me *Aluka,* the Hebrew word for leech. He knew what I was, and yet he stood there before me, unafraid, looking at me with eyes of sympathy, touching my heart with his compassion.

"We are all different in our own special ways," he said stroking the pink triangle on his chest. I could have kissed him, that kind, gentle, thoughtful, pretty, pretty boy.

"You would do that for me? You are not frightened of me?"

"Fear is something that should be reserved for that which is not understood. I have watched you, seen how you help. I think you have been sent here to help us."

"How could you possibly know that? You don't even know me, what I am capable of."

"I saw how you mourned your roommate. I saw the

sadness that his passing caused you, the pain that filled your eyes. No monster could feel such compassion."

I brought my hand up to touch his fingers resting on my shoulder and I squeezed them gently. The boy smiled at me, and it was a glorious smile, the warmest thing I had seen in that place, and my heart exploded with renewed faith. Perhaps there was still hope for mankind after all.

We started to unload the truck, working in pairs. I carried arms full of thick heavy rope while my partner carried the crucifixes. I was careful not to look at them, concentrating on his face, focussed on everything but the things in his hands. Yet that did not stop me from feeling twitchy and slightly spangled, as though I was working outside of my body, observing myself from a distance.

A routine quickly developed. He would hold the cross against the face of the box and I would wrap the rope around it, avoiding the touch of the offending shapes at all cost. But by the time we got to the fifth box, I was starting to feel dizzy, as everywhere I looked there were crosses, in front of me, behind me, to the side of me, burning into my soul with knowing purpose. I closed my eyes, but I could still see them, and I did not know how to get through it.

"Talk to me," he said, trying to keep me lucid.

"Your name," I gasped, "what is your name?"

"Joseph. My parents were not without a sense of humour."

I laughed despite myself, the sound chasing away the gut wrenching nausea eating away at my stomach. "I like it."

"It's a cliché, admit it."

"I wouldn't dare."

Joseph laughed a soft heart-warming sound. His face lit up when he laughed, washing away the horror that surrounded us, and for a moment I forgot myself. I stumbled against the crucifix we had just bound.

Blinding white light seared my eyes. Flames burst across my vision. I heard the clash of steel, the cries of anger and the agony of war. I felt that terrible wave of bitter disappointment crashing over me, accompanied by a deep, terrifying familial anger and I screamed from between tightly clenched lips.

His hands were upon me, pulling me away from the box, whispering kindness into my ear, the palms of his gentle fingers wiping away the tears that streamed from my eyes.

His touch calmed me and the nightmare faded. He made me feel safe.

"Come on, get on your feet, careful, lean on me, let me help you." He led me into a darkened corner, away from prying eyes, and gently pushed more rope into my hand, willing me on. "You can do this, take the rope and help me."

He was just a boy and I was ancient, yet the strength emanating from his soul penetrated me like the sun, healing my pain, purging the guilt that incapacitated me. I took the rope from him with shaking hands, unable to find the words to express my gratitude, amazed by his maturity, stunned by his humanity.

"Why does it affect you so badly? Crosses, I mean."

I tried to open my mouth, but my lips refused to work.

"It's okay—you don't have to tell me if you don't want to."

"No, I want to," I stammered, feeling returning to my lips. "The crucifix is a symbol of God and his son who died upon it. I am an affront to God, and therefore not permitted to look upon anything that directly relates to him."

"And sunlight? I thought you could not walk around in sunlight. Oh, and your reflection in a mirror, is that one true as well?" His enthusiasm almost made me smile.

"Sunlight is complicated. We are creatures of dark, we are born of darkness, and we commit dark deeds in order to stay alive. The sun drives out the dark. I however, am somewhat different."

"You can say that again."

His quip made me look up, but he averted his gaze, a slight flush colouring his cheeks. It made me smile. I liked him.

"As for mirrors, well, that one is true, for all of us. They say that the first of us, the first vampire, was so ashamed of what he was that his image vanished from his mirror so he could not gaze upon the thing that he had become. I however have another theory, that it is God who is ashamed of us, of what we are, and it is he who refuses to let us see ourselves."

"That's quite a loss in your case."

He was grinning from ear to ear, and I scowled at him playfully. His smirk slowly faded and he was serious again.

"Are you ashamed of what you are?"

"The vampire? Sometimes. The rest? No. Are you?"

"I was. When I told my parents they were so angry, so ashamed, disappointed. They do not understand what I am and therefore they are afraid of what I am. Religion is such a part of our people, bred into us at a very young age, so that anything that contradicts that faith is terrifying to them. They threw me out when I was sixteen."

I stopped and looked at him, that earnest, honest young man with more compassion than I had witnessed in a century, and I found myself admiring him.

"That must have been hard."

"It was, at first. But I had good friends and they made me realise that if God created man in his image, then God created me, and he made me what I am. He made you too."

"I seriously doubt that."

"Then if he didn't make you, who did?"

Who, indeed? "I don't know. I don't know who made

me."

"You know what I think? I think you can walk in daylight because God has not given up on you."

His words astounded me. Never had that thought even crossed my mind, dared to cross my mind. It made me inexplicably angry and I tried very carefully to temper my words, to blunt my inexplicable anger. He was just a child, what did he know?

"How can you of all people say that, here, now, in this place? Where is your God now, because he damn well isn't here helping his chosen ones, is he?" Harsh words and I knew it, but I needed to say them. No God, no compassionate all loving God, could allow such cruelty. I refused to believe that.

"It is not God that does this to us, it's man."

"How old are you?"

"Nineteen." He laughed. "How old are you?"

"Cheeky!"

"You should see me on a good day."

"There will be good days. I promise you that."

He looked at me then, his face a mask of desperation, of pleading, a face that so wanted to believe that I could deliver him from evil.

"Do you promise? Please promise me."

I moved with lightning speed and took him into my arms, holding him close to my chest, stroking his bald fuzzy head. He gripped me tightly, his thin body shivering in my grasp, his heart beating heavily against my chest. He smelled of youth and forgotten dreams, of misplaced hope and utter desperation, but also faith and strength, of burning desire, the desire to live.

"I promise you, with all my heart."

He disentangled himself from my arms and wiped away his tears with one hand while slapping me playfully on the chest with the other.

"You have no heart, remember?"

"Hey you cheeky brat, I have a heart, I just need to find it again."

His gaze bore into me. Big clear brown eyes that spoke of innocence, eyes that brimmed with the yearning to love.

"I think you have already found it." His lips trembled as he spoke.

Why then? Why such beauty in that place? Another time, another world, maybe there would have been a chance, but not there and not then. I was about to walk into darkness, into a world of monsters beyond his imagination, to confront an evil as ancient as civilisation itself, and I could not take him with me. I would not take him with me. But I would set him free.

The sky above us erupted as lightening ripped apart the sky. It was almost as though God knew what I was thinking. The clouds rippled with anger. Big fat drops of water exploded against our upturned faces, washing the grime away, and we stood there laughing into the sky, allowing the storm to wipe away our pain, a tiny moment of stolen joy in a world of undiluted misery.

As the rain started to intensify, the Kapos gathered us all together, screaming for us to fall into line. They grinned at each other slyly, looking very pleased with themselves. They huddled together whispering, then our Kapo let rip with a loud belly laugh, pointing at us. I felt Joseph's fingers brush against my hand, gently twining themselves around my knuckles, and I squeezed them reassuringly.

"Right, you little shit burglars and foreskin thieves, listen up. Our benevolent Blockfürher has seen fit to reward you for your hard work today. In a one-time only gesture, you get to use the officer's facilities, and that means a hot shower. Follow me."

They led us in silence to the farthest corner of the camp, which contained a solitary building, a long windowless, brick rectangle with a metal stairway leading up to its flat roof. A tall wall isolated the building from the rest of the camp. It looked more like a bomb shelter than a shower facility, a bomb shelter patrolled by armed guards both on the ground and above on the roof.

"Listen up faggots, you will take off your clothes and fold them onto the tables before you. There will be no touching and no cock sucking!" The Nazi soldiers burst out laughing. "Move!"

We began to disrobe. I had always been very aware of my body, my tight smooth skin, the hardness of my stomach rippling through my taught flesh, the muscular curve of my biceps and the plunging crevice of my hard pecks. I was a thing of magnificence. Never, never had I wished it to be otherwise. But as I glanced around me, at emaciated bodies, at skin that hung from bones, at dirty and bruised flesh, I felt deeply ashamed of my obvious beauty. I had always stood out in a crowd, and I relished the eyes that consumed me with utter adoration and desire, but for once in my pathetic existence, I did not want anyone to look at me. But they did.

They were trying not to. But I stood out like a sore thumb—you couldn't miss me. I felt their furtive glances brush across my skin, taking in my physique, my health. I was a walking talking corpse for fuck's sake, and I still looked healthier than they did. Their faces bore no evidence of accusation or even envy, and I was surprised to sense a fair amount of desire coming from some of them. You had to love the human spirit.

Joseph disrobed at my side and I nearly wept at the sight of his frail body. Ribs threatened to break through skin so tight I feared it would tear if I touched it. His hips stuck out sharp and pronounced, and his stomach was nothing but a

110

hollow inverted space. But he stood proud before me, unafraid and unashamed, his eyes drinking in every aspect of my body, every muscle, every curve. I thought for one heart-stopping moment he was going to reach out and touch me, that his fingers would trace a path down through the valley of my chest, across the mountains of my abs, but he didn't, and the feeling of disappointment that washed over me hurt. He smiled at me and I smiled down at him, David and Goliath, joined together in our shared wretchedness, bound by our new found friendship, bound by our need to find some form of humanity in that hellish pit of despair.

It took two men to open the huge metal doors of the bunker that shared the same dull colour as the grey storm clouds above, tainted by patchy spider-webbed tendrils of red-brown rust that radiated across the pitted surfaces. Each man pulled on a lever, one on each door, straining with all their insignificant might against the rusted steel, their muscles bulging through their heavy uniforms, their faces contorted with effort. They looked as though they were trying to squeeze one out. With a complaining groan of steel against steel, the levers began to move, a screech of metal that sliced through the night and particles of red rust the colour of dried blood burst from the encrusted surface of the locking mechanism to drift to the floor, mixing with the rainwater in a pool of liquid decay.

The titanic steel doors opened outward, their massive hinges screaming like tortured souls, sending a cold chill down my spine that ended in an uneasy knot in the pit of my stomach. I felt the hairs on my arms prickle, each one standing on end in protest, in warning, crying out to me that everything in front of me was wrong.

I wondered what the fuck they had in there. King Kong?

Someone somewhere threw a switch. I heard it, my keen vampire ears picking up the buzz of a circuit completing.

Sparks flew from overhead wires and transformers in a cascade of glittering particles as electricity surged through insulated copper. The air buzzed with ozone. Blackness exploded into blinding white light and we all raised our hands to shield our eyes from its intensity.

"In you go, you filthy bastards—in you go for your nice hot shower." I looked at the Kapo, my eyes burning with defiance and hatred, willing my fury to destroy him, to reduce him to a pile of filthy ashes. But he stood his ground and met my gaze, a smirk creasing the corners of his vile mouth while the surrounding Nazis laughed.

Like animals entering the Ark, we walked toward the light, two by two, and I gripped Joseph's hand tightly as the surrounding bodies swallowed us. I could feel his pulse pounding through his skin and hear his heart banging against his chest. All around me the cacophony of beating hearts rose to a fever pitched crescendo, the smell of raw fear pervading all. Lions to the slaughter, we all felt it. Yet we walked forward, unable to prevent it, unable to turn back, unable to resist the light that drew us in like moths to a flame.

We found ourselves in a long rectangular room lined with cold white tiles. Lime-scale-encrusted showerheads pierced the tiles at regular intervals, and harsh glowing bulbs illuminated the grim space from within steel cages bolted directly to the ceiling. Four large metal hatches punctuated the ceiling, their handless metal surfaces dulled with age.

The smell was so malodorous I could taste it. The chamber reeked of age-old disinfectant and bleach, the air itself stale and heavy, the rank taste on my tongue intensifying with every breath, every nuance of every odour distinct to my vampire nose. Underneath the overbearing smell of hospital lay something else, something that only I could detect, a scent unmasked by the heady layers of ancient disinfectant, a scent that assaulted my nose with its odious presence, the unmistakable smell of death. It clung to every tile and dripped from the ceiling in thick striations of overwhelming grief, violent and indiscriminate.

Suddenly the metal doors slammed closed behind us, filling our white coffin with a loud foreboding clang. The portentous creak of the heavy locking mechanism sliding into place followed instantly.

I didn't know what was happening and I didn't know what to do. I looked into their faces, awash with fear and confusion, and I could offer no comfort. Any last remnant of hope seemed to melt away from their bodies and I felt the weight of their sorrow and their despair slice through my heart like a blade.

I had never felt so useless.

And then something extraordinary happened. Joseph took both of my hands in his brittle fingers, cradling them so gently in his fragile grip, and I felt his thumbs caressing the backs of my hands in soft circular motions that sent a thrill through my skin. I looked into his pretty face and saw tears streaming down his ashen cheeks. There was such a look of profound sadness about him it made me want to cry, and I didn't know why, I didn't know what was happening. Something clouded his eyes, something like resignation and loss, yet he still managed the smallest of smiles, the smallest of smiles that he gave to me. And then he started to sing.

The voice that trilled through his trembling lips was the sweetest sound I had ever heard. It was the sound of a morning birdsong greeting the rising sun—it was the scent of a flower unfurling its glory to the world, it was the sound of joy given birth by that one true angel born of Heaven. And I could see the angels weeping at the sound, I could hear God himself shifting uneasily as that voice, the voice of a mere child, flew through his own grief, through his own sadness, touching my darkened soul so profoundly I felt my own cold tears spill from my eyes and fall on my skin.

God needed to sit up and take notice.

The others began to take up the Hebrew prayer, their voices united as hands reached out to link into another until the white room soared with the sound of music, their voices fighting through their terror. It was a sound so moving as to chase away the prevailing terror, to banish it from the corners of the earth, soaring in a concord of perfect harmony. Men of different ages, men of contradictory beliefs, of different needs, singing together in one prayer, joined as one people across tides of adversity and conflict. Discrimination, differences, arguments, forgotten on a tide of joined voices. Just men, taking solace in one another, finding comfort with other men.

The sound was so profound, the emotion that it instilled felt so deeply, so pure, so haunting and while I did not understand their words, I felt their meaning. I felt the tenderness and the sentiment their words portrayed and I basked in the humanity they gave of themselves so generously and so selflessly. I realised then, at that moment, in that place, what it meant to be human. What destroyed them just made them stronger, what tore them apart simply united them, that persecution just made them love unconditionally.

To love was to hurt, and to hurt was to be human.

With a loud clang, the hatches above our heads opened and four smoking parcels fell from the sky, the hatches closing instantly behind them. White smoke hissed and billowed from the parcels that exploded across the floor, releasing a fine white powder that seemed to react upon contact with the air, turning the powder into a dense white cloud of noxious gas.

But they continued to sing, their voices rising in volume,

trembling but resolute.

The gas began to fill the room, thick white columns of billowing, acrid plumes that stung even my dead flesh. A man near an exploded parcel screamed in abject terror as blood began to pour from the corners of his eyes. The scream began to gurgle in his throat as thick white foam bubbled from his open mouth. He collapsed to the floor, his body twitching violently against the tiles, flesh slapping against the cold harsh ceramic surface like a gasping fish on a marble slab.

"Close your eyes, Joseph, for the love of God, close your eyes."

All around me the sound of agony, screams that could drive you into the arms of insanity and yet Joseph continued to sing, his one clear voice ringing above the frantic sounds of death. I saw fingers gouging at eyes, ripping at skin that blistered and shredded beneath the onslaught of frenzied nails. I was plummeting through Hell as all those around me began to fall.

"Cover your mouth, Joseph, cover your nose and mouth, don't breathe it in, please don't breath it in!"

I flew at the heavy metal doors using my body as a battering ram. My shoulder exploded in agonising pain as it collided with the metal, bone snapping with a loud crack that ripped through my body. But I ignored the pain and began to hammer at the surface of the door with my bare fists. I felt my rage surging through my body, I felt my vampire erupt from my being and tear at the metal with all my terrible strength, but the door refused to buckle beneath the relentless onslaught of my wrath, solid, immutable.

Men fell, one by one crumpling to the floor, bodies contorted in death, blood pouring from their eyes, foam spurting in thick frothy fountains from between blue lips. I was running out of time.

I leaped onto the ceiling and scuttled toward the nearest hatch. The sounds of death and pain threatened to overwhelm me, to swallow me in their despair as their dying cries tore at the fabric of my being, shattering my sanity. I hammered with my fists, clawed at the metal with my useless talons, desperate for my hands to peel back the metal, to create an opening, but there was nothing there for me to grip, not a crack, not an edge. It was hopeless. I screamed and bellowed at the steadfast metal. I ripped, I tore, and I thrashed at the steel until my hands grew bloody and ragged, yet we remained trapped within that white coffin, sealed against a world that cared not for our fate.

I dropped to the floor just as Joseph turned around, his legs unsteady, his skin dusted with a fine coating of white powder. Blood tears dripped from the corners of his tightly closed eyes, and as he opened them to look at me, I saw they were red and filled with blood. But even through his agony he saw me, his eyes, once so pale and so innocent, looked upon the vampire and he saw me, the real me. His lips twitched upward trying to smile, a weak futile gesture that shattered my already broken heart, and a torrent of red tinged foam spewed from between his ischaemic lips.

"No!"

Suddenly he stumbled, falling forward, and I rushed to catch him in my open arms.

"No!" The word exploded from my lips with such ferocity as to shatter the world. Joseph fell into my arms and I lowered him gently to the floor, pulling his shattered body closer to my chest, cradling his poor naked body that withered before my very eyes. I could see his strength leaving as his life began to fade. Joseph was dying.

"You are... beautiful," he gasped, the words gurgling from the back of his throat, seeping between lips that were gorged with blood.

"Stay with me, Joseph, please stay with me." The words caught in my throat, I could barely speak them, and all around me horror, mindless horror that left me numb. And that life, that precious, young beautiful life, fading in my arms, all hope, all potential, extinguished through an act of absolute evil. It was too much for my mind to take.

"I promised you, do you remember? I promised..."

His hand brushed my cheek, tracing the outline of my vampire face, sliding down to feel the sharpness of my teeth against my trembling lips.

"Will... will you do something... for me?" His voice faltering as his body shuddered.

"Please," I sobbed, "anything."

"Let me see... let me see you... one last time."

I did not give voice to the wail that reached my lips, at the overwhelming pain that exploded with such furious anger through every fibre of my body. My head spun from side to side, eyes desperately searching, begging for help, pleading for help, for that torture, for that hell to end, but there was nothing, just agony and blood and the dying of innocents.

I pulled my vampire back. He looked at me then, his sweet face at peace, then his head lolled back and his hands fell limp to the floor.

"No!" My rage screamed from my body in a tempest of unbridled fury. My head reared back, the roar ripping through my mouth, my teeth slashing down to meet the flesh of Joseph's throat, slicing through his thin flesh. I forced myself to suck in great mouthfuls of his poisoned blood, spitting it out, repeating the process again and again, thick red viscous fluid exploded across my face and my chest as I gulped mouthful after mouthful, an inhuman, insane animal. Then my wrist at my mouth, my teeth ripping at my own flesh, tearing at the artery, my blood erupting over my body, a crimson spray, and I rammed the bloodied wound into Josephs mouth, pressing my wrist against his cold unmoving lips.

"Drink, Joseph. Drink," I pleaded with that cold dead thing, my teeth tearing at my bottom lip, but his lips did not move.

"Let me save you, Joseph." Words, useless, dead, pointless.

My tears poured onto his dead face, my body shivering with grief.

"Please let me save you."

Joseph was dead. Dead hands, dead eyes. Dead. And I could not bring him back. I could not save him. I scooped his dead mangled body into my arms, clutching him tightly to my chest, rocking his corpse back and forth, my sobs the only sound in that cold white tomb. I let my grief pour over me, let my sorrow tear away my world, for it was a world consumed by unspeakable darkness, a world full of despair, a world that was broken, a world without Joseph.

And I wept in a sea of the dead.

Chapter Twenty-two: Death Camp Six

As related by Malachi

What a bizarre parade of fetish freaks. Weird, grotesque walking corpses with squirming squid things stuck to their necks. Eww. The sight of them made me want to chuck. And as for the two lanky leather queens, what was that all about? Really, way to overdo leather. All that lascivious lip, tongue, eye contact action, please, get a room.

Eli, the daft fuck, he nearly gave the game away. I knew he needed to feed but really—he needed to get a grip, for both our sakes and fast.

Find Isaiah. Rescue Isaiah. Set prisoners free. I liked to think of it as the IIF manoeuvre. Mind you, the entire bloody thing was iffy, if you asked me. What we would not do for a pretty face and a hard set of abs?

It took hours to remove all the boxes from the cargo containers, and by the time we carried the last ones away, my feet were bloody killing me. Hob nailed boots should be banned. I needed a good foot massage, and I had the overwhelming desire for a nice cup of tea and a chocolate bourbon.

A sudden shove against my shoulder dispelled my pleasant ruminations of tea and biscuits.

"Well go on then, you daft twat, you heard him."

I glared at Stefan with as much manly indignation as I could muster—I radiated manliness. "Is there any need?"

"So help me God, I'm gonna give you what for if you

don't pull yourself together and get in there... so help me God."

"It would help if I knew what the fuck you were on about, my man!"

"Bodies, in the cargo containers. He told you to remove them and take them to the morgue. Jesus Christ. You've been acting dead queer since you came back."

A smirk threatened to crease my lips. If only he knew. Though why our grand Blockfürher instructed *me* to remove the bodies, I did not know. Did I look like a mortician? But I had the sneaky suspicion that my appalling attention span had resulted in Stefan pulling a blinder, sneaky, ugly gimp.

"And pray what, may I ask, will you be doing while I'm sweating my bollocks off?"

Stefan screwed up his fist and made a show of drilling it into my forehead. Never thought I'd see the day when Stefan fisted me.

"I'll be the one bringing in the flatbed, see. You do all the brawn and I will do all the thinking. Stupid."

With feet that sung *kum bay ya,* I trudged over to the nearest empty car, slinging my rifle carelessly over my right shoulder. The butt of the rifle whipped up and hit me under my chin, nearly knocking my teeth out of my startled mouth, and a loud guffaw erupted from behind me. I cringed with embarrassment. The little bastard missed nothing.

"See what I mean?" His laughter infuriated me.

Cunt. "Fuck off." Without waiting to see his cocky expression or listen to what I was sure would be another sparkling witticism, I spun around on my heels to face the awaiting cargo freighter and pulled myself up into the gapping black hole.

Bugger me, it was so dark in there. Eww, and the smell. I felt my morning's feast of half a packet of bourbons churn in the pit of my stomach, and my mouth stung with the acid taste of bile. It stunk of poo.

My human eyes found it difficult to penetrate the gloom. The straw littered floor felt thick and heavy underfoot, matted with something sticky and horrible that I had absolutely no desire to identify. Rough planks of wood lined the walls, many baring scars, claw marks raked into their splintered surface. Someone needed a manicure.

Out of the corner of my eye, I glimpsed something glistening black slumped on the floor against the far wall, and I found myself squinting through the gloom, my feeble human eyes unable to focus. My host needed glasses. I could have simply walked over there and looked, but I was terrified, my legs trembling, my feet glued to the wood floor. It must have been all that poo.

I craned my neck forward, trying to see, but at the same time not really wanting to. A foot, I could just make out a shiny booted foot sticking out at a funny angle from beneath something glossy, perhaps a leather trench coat.

Something soft collided with the back of my legs and I screamed like a bitch, a big loud girly scream. Fay Wray would have been so proud.

"You'll need that, to cover the body. The boss doesn't want anyone seeing the bodies." My heart thumped wildly inside my chest. The figure leaning in through the opening pointed at the blanket, but then my eyes decided to work perfectly and I could see his shoulders jiggling with laughter. "Nice scream by the way," he quipped as he walked away.

I picked up the grey blanket and shook off the bits of straw, the fabric itchy between my fingers. Eww. Wool.

I kept telling myself I could do it, that I should pull myself together and just do it. Just run over there, throw the blanket over the nice corpse before dragging his carcass out of there. A couple of times I even jerked forward, but then quickly leaped back, skipping from foot to foot with the itchy blanket tossing between my indecisive hands.

"Okay, this is it, blanket, body, out. Marvellous." I darted forward and threw the cloth over the slumped body.

Something moved in my peripheral vision. I slapped my hands against my mouth with such force I nearly knocked myself out, fighting the scream of absolute horror that perched precariously on my terrified lips, but I held it there tightly. There was a figure standing in the dark with his back to me.

"Stefan?" I knew it wasn't Stefan before the word squeaked timidly from my lips. The figure was wearing shiny black hobnail boots and a long glistening leather trench coat, the *same* uniform as the body underneath the grey, cringe-inducing wool cloth. And I could see straight through him.

You go for years without seeing a single ghost and now I was positively drowning in them.

I moved around him slowly, creeping to the side so I could see his face, but just as I got into position, his head turned toward me. His mouth opened in a terrible silent scream, tearing his face in two. And then he blinked out of existence.

"Quit fucking about in there and drag that poor sod out will you?" Stefan's voice made me jump, but for once, I was grateful to hear his gruff voice. Something about that ghost disturbed me, and something was stirring deep inside my dead brain, some fragment, some splinter of a memory, a connection. It frightened me.

I grabbed the ankles of the fallen SS soldier and dragged him toward the light. He was a heavy bugger.

"Don't be such a fucking wimp, haul that carcass over here."

I swung around, my hands on my hips and glared at

Stefan. "If you think you could do any better, then get your hairy ass in here."

"Bet you'd like that, faggot."

"Don't be such a fool, Stefan." His quip rankled, which surprised me. The body I inhabited was a hardened soldier, used to the rigours of warfare and manual labour, my host's firm muscular body a testament to his manhood. I, on the other hand, was a raving homosexual who could barely float without mincing. I had tried very hard to act butch in that body, but the queen was leeching through. And Stefan saw that.

In an attempt to underline my manliness, I grabbed the body with renewed purpose and astounded myself by pulling it to the threshold of the container with little effort. Adrenalin was a wonderful thing when mixed with a queen's wrath. I literally threw the legs of the cadaver at Stefan's face, and he had to duck away to avoid the heavy boots from kicking his already mashed face.

"Stick that in your flatbed and suck it." I felt my lips pucker into a pout. I could not help it.

I jumped down, glad to be out of that claustrophobic slaughterhouse and I stormed over to the flatbed truck where two more bodies lay sprawled in the back, grey sheets covering them from prying eyes. I climbed into the passenger seat of the small green vehicle, slamming the door closed behind me.

"Hey you fuck, you going to help me with this lump or what?" Stefan bellowed indignantly through the open window.

"You're such a man, move it your bloody self."

I sat there defiantly with my arms crossed, staring furiously ahead for what seemed like eons. The truck lurched and the suspension squealed as something heavy thudded onto the back, then the driver's door swung open with a loud screech.

"Fucking twat." He turned the key and fought with the gear stick. The gearbox made a very loud, very rude noise and I suppressed a smirk as Stefan swore under his breath. I thought all *men* could drive.

I stared out of the mud-flecked windshield, but my eyes saw nothing. My mind raced away to another place, to another time, piecing parts of my puzzle together, trying to make sense of all I had learned.

How did I die? I couldn't remember who I was or where I was from. I spoke with an English accent and I loved a good cup of tea, so obviously I was English. Also, I must have died an extraordinary death, something unusual, uncommon, something so out of the realms of my human experience and so far removed from my understanding, as to wipe it from my consciousness. Traumatic and out of the ordinary, it sounded just like me.

The ghosts in the incinerator room, they all wore the same thing, the stripped uniforms in which they had died, and the spirit of the SS soldier I had glimpsed in the cargo hold—he wore the same uniform in which he died.

Therefore, I was wearing the clothes in which I died.

I had never really stopped to think about it before. It didn't mean anything to me. They were just clothes. Had I given it more thought, if I had allowed the idea to gestate, then maybe I would have seen it, the suspicion lurking in the dark recesses of my mind, but I had just refused to see it, refused to give it credence because they were, after all, just clothes? And what did clothes prove?

My vest or waistcoat, to use the modern vernacular, was a rich red silk affair embroidered with a black oriental design, a common theme back then. Then there was my crisp white shirt with its separate collar and cuffs, suitable for both formal and informal occasions. Laundering was not so common back in the day, so that was an essential requirement of any gentleman's wardrobe. My lovely grey trousers with the thinnest of black pin stripes buttoned up to just below my navel. I always loved the way the flat front of my pants accentuated my package. I dressed to the right. And then of course, there was my lovely black frock coat, fitted snugly to my waistline at my own insistence, with a full skirt at the front and back that reached just above my knees. Oh, I knew the sack suit had long been in fashion, cut as the name suggested, as a large loosely fitted, shapeless box. I was having none of that. Definition was the name of the game.

I clutched my head. It was all too much. Too many thoughts and memories, all flooding in at once, shattering my happy little world. I wanted to tear the little van apart with my own bare hands, to feel the metal ripping and disintegrating between my fingers. My anger and my rage threatened to consume me in a burning cataclysm of fury. Too much, too much pain and I did not, could not face it.

"Help me take them into the morgue."

I nodded, my lips unable to move, my eyes bulging with a grief I did not understand and I did not want.

"You're very quiet."

"I've got a lot on my mind."

"You haven't got a fucking mind, you little faggot."

I saw red. Something inside me snapped. All my anger, all my frustration, all the fears percolating through my head exploded against him as I gripped him by the shoulders and slammed him into the side of the van, my face a snarling fury of teeth and spittle. I heard him yelp in pain as his back collided against the metal with a loud crunch, but I did not care, nor did I care about the look of shock and fear that suddenly appeared on his ugly face, fear of me, of my anger, of my blossoming demon. My voice, angry and unfamiliar to me, roared into his face in a torrent of spittle and phlegm.

"If I wanted to suck a cock then I would have to look for a real man, wouldn't I, so I guess that rules you out, you ugly piece of fucking shit!"

The demon inside me grew and grew. It was all I could do to suppress it. If Stefan saw that side of me, even glimpsed the yellow that burned in my eyes, I would have to kill him. I would enjoy killing him. I looked forward to killing him.

I released his throat and he slumped to the floor gasping, his hands held up in supplication. No more doubts about my manhood there.

"Now help me move these bodies into the morgue." I leaned into the back of the van and slung a body effortlessly over my shoulder. With a last derisive sneer at my cowering comrade, I stalked away into the small brick building.

My strength started to ebb as my anger waned. I felt like I was standing on the edge of a precipice looking down upon my own damnation. Never had I come so close to understanding what had happened to me. It hurt, really bloody hurt. The thought that I could know, that the truth, my truth, was so close to me I could touch it, terrified me. After so many years with Eli, so many strange but happy years, I felt as though that time was coming to a close. That to find myself would mean losing him, and I no longer knew which was more important to me, finding my identity, or staying with Eli.

I slung the body on top of a large stainless steel table that lay in the middle of the room. A sterile white room of sparkling tiles and glittering implements it was not. Grime coated the walls. Heavy dust laden cobwebs festooned the dark corners in great swathes of gossamer strands and long, dripping, rusty brown arches of dried blood splashed across the brick walls and flagstone floor. It made my stomach churn. Next to the central table sat a grubby trolley displaying a set of dirtied implements, a large encrusted bone saw, a couple of stained scalpels and a rather evil looking set of pliers.

Stefan stumbled heavily into the room with a corpse across his shoulder, looking like he was about to collapse under its weight, but I did not help him. I watched with some satisfaction as he struggled to dump the body on the table.

"There is one more," he mumbled, his eyes unable to meet my own.

"Then get it."

I walked around the crude examination table, gazing at the shrouded lumps of ex-humanity that lay discarded before me. I felt something crunch beneath my boot. I had stood on a fingernail, the bloodied root still clinging to the keratin. I nearly threw up

Morgue my fucking ass.

And still my clothes haunted me. I died in those clothes, clothes of a by-gone era.

The door slammed violently against the brick wall, throwing up a cloud of dust as Stefan carried in the last corpse. Sweat poured from him, staining his uniform in all the nastiest places. I bet that was beginning to chafe — served his own bloody right.

"You... can get... the rings," he spat from between clenched teeth as he lowered the body onto the table. The metal legs squealed in complaint.

"I beg your pardon?"

For a moment, I saw the sarcastic comment sit on his lips, almost given voice, but his face quickly changed tack and I noted with much satisfaction how carefully he tempered his reply.

"Our grand Blockfürher has another job he needs me to do right away, I got to go and help a detail clean out a couple of recently vacated bunkers." He laughed at this as though he expected me to understand and join in with his little joke. I didn't have a clue what he was laughing at.

"Anyway," he continued rather awkwardly, "someone has to take the Death Head rings off of these three and take them up to the castle. It's an SS tradition."

"Okay." He looked at me long and hard then, his eyes searching my own as though he were looking for something.

"You have changed, you know," he said gently. "You used to love my jokes, you used to understand them, you knew that it was all a front, you know..."

"No, I don't know." I could barely conceal my irritation. I just wanted him gone.

"Did you mean what you said? When you called me ugly?" I shrugged non-committed. "So does that mean it's over, then?"

Well I didn't see that coming. My host and that man, boyhood friends, thrust together under the most difficult of circumstances, forced to perform the most horrendous of duties, compelled to witness the most obscene atrocities. How their humanity twisted. How their sanity was tested. It was no wonder then, that they sought solace, the only solace they could find, with one another.

They say that those who shout the loudest have the most to hide.

I didn't know what to say to him. What could I say—that I wasn't really his boyfriend, that I was just a spirit borrowing his lover's body for a top-secret mission. Oh, and that, by the way, you are German—don't you burn homosexuals?

The complexity of humankind astonished me. The hypocrisy of our race, it sickened me.

Stefan turned away and walked dejectedly toward the door and I felt my conscience twang.

"Stefan..." He looked at me over his shoulder and I was surprised to see his eyes glistened with tears. "I'll see you later, I promise." The smile that flickered over his lumpy, misshaped face showed relief, and I let him go without another word. When I left my host, then they could work things out, nothing more to do with me.

If I left my host.

I stared down at the three corpses, gripping the edge of the cold stainless steel table so hard my knuckles turned white. The room spun and I fought against the urge to close my eyes and allow the calamity of my existence to swallow me up in darkness. Those dead lumps of cold hard flesh lying before me screamed in my face, imploring me to wipe the shit from my eyes and smell the roses, to make that final leap of painful logic. But something in my head prevented me from attaining that final moment of clarity, pushing me back from the brink of that chasm with all its cruel might, refusing to reach the revelation that was cresting on the horizon of my consciousness.

Unsteady hands reached out and pulled back the first blanket, not really wanting to see the dead thing beneath, but I felt compelled all the same. The face that greeted me was a twisted rictus of pure terror and pain, the mouth open in the last breath of some terrible scream, and on the right side of his neck a bloodied wound, two ragged puncture marks glowering back at me, daring me to see them.

My body began to shiver. Such anger I had never known before, a deep rage that inflamed my nerves, setting them on fire, twisting my features into a snarl of utter pain and fury. I ripped the remaining sheets from the table to reveal two more mutilated corpses, drained of life, with faces that would never again know peace.

My face felt wet. Tears poured down my flush cheeks. Sorrow and pain ripped at my soul, a hurt so profound I wanted to die, to cease my existence there and then. I would have done anything to remove myself from the trauma of blossoming memory. But my sorrow was not for those lifeless lumps of meat before me — my tears did not belong to them.

Bones cracked and splintered as I ripped the Death Head rings from their stiff fingers, but I did not care, all I heard was my wailing, the pathetic sound of mourning pouring from my lips in unstoppable grief, grief that was for me.

I knew they were there. They had been there for quite some time, the three spectres with their faces to the wall. Anger flared hot and un-tempered in my veins and I wanted to piss on them, to burn them with the full force of my bitterness, with the flames of Hell itself, to smite them from my sight.

How dare they make me confront such horror?

How dare they make me remember?

"Look at them!" I screamed, my voice cracking with emotion that threatened to burn me. I was a tempest, unfettered and raw, powerful.

"Look at them! See how you died!"

Slowly, the spirits turned and looked down upon their cold dead corpses lying on the slab, empty, blank faces staring at their own death.

I needed them to see. I needed them to understand. *I* needed to understand.

"Look at what they did to you," I shouted, unable to tame... not wanting to tame... the demon that grew inside me. "Look at how you died, how they defiled your bodies, how they sucked you dry, how they killed you, without mercy, without remorse! Remember!" My bitterness could sever flesh.

Slowly, painfully, it came back to them as one by one they remembered. I saw the pain of it wash over their faces in waves of revulsion, the memory of death ripping at their throats, draining their lives. Dull eyes opened with horror, the slow understanding of the damned. The moment was blinding, almost euphoric and I relished it, I felt the cruel satisfaction of their dawning memories, the violence of their deaths, the brutality of their murder creep over my face with a smile. And all the while, the tears continued to pour down my face, tears of my own despair.

And with a blaze of comprehension, the walls around my mind fell down and my memories flooded back with uncompromising ferocity. I crumpled to my knees as the agony of the oncoming storm tore through my mind with remorseless intent and I wept until my body had no more water to shed. It felt as if a veil lifted from my eyes and I could finally see with razor sharp clarity, a sharpness that cut into every organ of my body and sliced the skin from my bone, flaying through a new layer of flesh with every new memory.

How could I have been so stupid? How could I have been so naïve?

My life as an actor flashed before my eyes in all its cruel glory. The love of the stage that had so consumed me in life lay forgotten in death. How could I forget about that? How could I forget the battle with my parents over my career choice, one of many such arguments, fighting against their bitter disappointment and shame for not following my father's example? A lawyer's life was not for me, I had pleaded, I wanted to be an actor — I lived to entertain people, not sue them. Oh how my father had shouted at me. Acting was no serious profession, full of degenerates and perverts. If only they had known. But as it turned out, that argument never transpired, because my life ended at the moment of my greatest triumph.

That last night at the Lyceum Theatre was a precious,

beautiful memory, because I proved my parents wrong that night. I had landed the lead role in King Lear, and we were about to finish the most successful run the Lyceum had ever seen. I had become the toast of London, the name that was on everyone's lips and the darling of the tabloid critics. However, my parents refused to acknowledge my success despite the glowing reviews that I left open so diligently on the dining room table every breakfast. Their son was a star in the ascendance, but they eclipsed me with their disapproval. Until, that was, on closing night.

I think it must have been mother. I had heard them argue the night before, and they never argued, so they came — he came — out of love for her, for my mother.

As I stood on that stage on that perfect night, the atmosphere in the theatre was electric. There was a sense that something was about to be unleashed, that when the curtain opened the eyes of the whole world would be upon me for that final performance, that something truly magical was about to be created before the audiences very eyes. I had never been so nervous, or so excited. The offers were already pouring in and I knew that when the curtain fell on that final act, I would be able to take my pick of the juiciest rolls in theatre. I had arrived.

The curtain parted to such silence that I thought the audience to be holding their breaths! Never had a performance been met by such expectation! And then I saw them, my mother and father, sitting in the front row, staring up at that gas lit stage, staring up at me, their son.

I froze. The room darkened, but all I could see were my parents, looking at me. For a split second, just that one fleeting moment, I thought my lips would not part to deliver the opening lines. So shocked was I to see them there. But then my mother gave me an encouraging nod, just the slightest of movements, the kindest of little smiles and I knew that all would be well. Something inside me ignited. I was alive with words that flowed from my lips like living poetry, and so began the performance of my life.

I came to my last speech, my dying speech, the audience in the palm of my hand, breathless with anticipation, and I saw that even my father was on the edge of his seat. My mother, bless her, had a handkerchief in her hand dabbing her eyes.

"And my poor fool is hanged! No, no, no life
"Why should a dog, a horse, a rat, have life,
"And thou no breath at all? Thou'lt come no more,
"Never, never, never, never, never!
"Pry you undo this button sir: thank you, sir
"Do you see this? Look on her, look, her lips,
"Look there, look there!"
And I died.

The crowd leaped to their feet, the sound of their clapping and the roar of their cries threatening to lift the rooftop off its trusses. That had never happened before, not at that point, the play was not over. Albany had yet to deliver his closing speech, but the audience was going wild, and my poor fellow actors looked so perplexed, trying desperately to finish the play, but the audience was having none of it.

My parents were on their feet clapping and screaming at the stage, and for the first time in my life, I felt that they saw me, really saw me. My mother wept openly, no longer able to stave the flood of tears that poured down her face, but my father, my father looked at me through wide eyes filled with awe and pride, pride for me.

My poor fellow actors gave up, lifted me into their arms, holding me aloft like a trophy for the adoring crowds to see. The theatre erupted with renewed vigour, the sounds of feet banging on the floor rocking the interior like multiple claps of thunder, and I didn't want it to end. The vision of my parents crying and cheering filled me with happiness, and I felt my own hot tears spring from my eyes, tears of pure joy.

Fifteen curtain calls. How could a human being keep clapping for that long? Never before in the history of the Lyceum had a performance received fifteen curtain calls. I thought I could die happy then. How happy was I?

As the curtain plummeted for the final time, my parents rushed back stage and flew into my arms in an embrace I hoped would never end. They encased me in love, real honest heartfelt love. I was their son and they were proud of me, proud of *me!*

I felt too wired to go home, and for the first time ever, my parents actually encouraged me to go out with my friends, proclaiming quite loudly that their star of a son should celebrate his newfound fame. Well, who was I to argue? Had I known that was our last moments together, the last time that I would ever kiss them, embrace them, I would not have left their sides. I should have gone home with them that night, back to the safety of our modest suburban home and the safety of my bed. I never said goodbye. I never told them how much I loved them. I never said thank you.

When did they die? Where was their resting place? Did my body lie with them?

My heart was breaking.

London offered but one haven for the likes of me, the Damnation Club, or DC as we fondly called it. DC was a very well-kept secret known only to a select circle of people in the know. Activities and tastes of my predilection were strictly against the law in Victorian London. Therefore, we lived an underground life, away from prying eyes and away from the constabulary. Membership to the Damnation Club was strictly by invitation only then only at the behest of a member.

Eli first introduced me to the club.

I loved the place, so filled to the brim with opulent excess. Men dressed as exuberant women put on outrageous satirical shows, and women dressed in men's eveningwear, immaculate and simply gorgeous. Sometimes it was hard to tell them apart—some of the women would have made exquisite looking men. At DC, I could relax, without the fear of discovery. I was an actor and I could act like any other heterosexual male, or so I thought, but the pretence wore thin very quickly, I liked men and that was the end of it. At DC, I could kiss a man without the fear of incarceration, and private rooms were available should I wish the evening's entertainment to escalate. But that night, I just wanted to drink, to drown in my success and the acceptance of my beloved family. I also required the sting of Absinth to help me forget the handsome bastard who had introduced me to that decadent world in the first place. I had fallen in love, but he had made it perfectly clear that it was a love unrequited.

Damn those memories, so vividly re-enacted in my mind's eye, visiting their pain upon me with such livid acuteness.

No amount of sweet nectar dripping from a sugar cube could wipe Eli out of my thoughts, and with precious little talent in the club that night, I decided to try my favourite cruising ground. I felt like being naughty.

As I left, I had a quiet word in the ear of one of DC's most loyal patrons, a rather large, sweaty man, who relished the company of young chickens. He had made a pass at me once but I was having none of it, and I think he admired me for that. We had been friends ever since. It also helped that he was the Police Commissioner. My favourite cruising ground when DC failed to fulfil my insatiable needs lay beneath London Bridge, frequented by horny sailors who did not care where they stuck it. The area was a known hot spot, frequently raided by the police, but my chunky friend assured me that another raid would not take place that night. So with my loins stirring with excitement at the prospect of something Russian... how I loved their thick... accents... and with quite a few shots percolating through my veins, I skipped away into the night to find my sailor.

The smell of London by night came back to me in thick delicious instalments. I remembered the ever-present smell of filthy water, the choking smell of coal and ash, an everyday by-product of such a heavily industrialised city. It was strange how the memory of a smell could stir up so many forgotten memories.

It was very late—or very early—and soon the streets would start to bustle with market traders as they began their long shift at dawn's crack. I hurried down onto the embankment, the thought of burly Russians taking me every-which-way spurring me on. But then I saw *him,* slumped against the wall in a pool of mud, holding his head in his hands, his shoulders heaving violently with every sob that wracked his fit muscular body.

I had never seen him like that. The sight of his sorrow so open to the world like a gaping wound pained me, and my feelings for him took flight in my heart once more. They said that the poisoned air of London was the greatest killer of the Victorian age, but I had to disagree. Love was.

"Eli. What has happened to you, for the love of God, what is wrong?" I knelt in the mud at his side, my hand tentatively reaching out to run my trembling fingers through his thick hair.

"Get away from me." He sounded so broken. I should have listened to him, fucking hindsight. But my obsession with him, with that creature of such dazzling beauty, drove me on.

"Please, let me help you, please tell me what it is that has hurt you so."

He moved so fast that my eyes could barely see. He crouched before me in all his vampire magnificence, his long teeth glistening against his lower lip, his eyes burning with terrible ferocity and pain. And still I did not retreat.

"This is not like you, Eli, you know me. We are friends, are we not?" I held my hands up in supplication, and like a fool I walked toward him, trying to keep my voice as reassuring as I could, trying to pacify the beast, but the animal before me was beyond reasoning. I saw it in his face, in his black eyes. I saw it too late.

I knew in that fleeting moment before death that I was a fool. I was a fool to think that I could love him. I was a fool to think that he could love me. I was a prize twat for thinking I could tame the monster that always lurked beneath the rock-hard surface of his body. I thought that night was going to be the start of everything for me. The start of an incredible career. The start of a fabulous life. I was a fool to think so.

I turned to run, a futile gesture. He took flight and landed before me, snarling, bestial. He was out of control, broken, a savage, an uncontrollable, ravenous beast beyond reasoning, and no amount of pleading would alter the course of his actions.

"But I love you, Eli."

I remembered a mass of claws and teeth, his terrible furious breath against the skin of my neck. I remembered him pawing at my skin like some dog burying a bone. I remembered hearing the sound of my own throat tearing at the touch of sharp, pitiless teeth, and the sound of him gulping down my blood as it pumped into his hungry mouth. And I remembered his eyes as the blackness began to seep across the edges of my vision, black merciless spheres of utter despair and hopelessness.

Eli killed me. I died at the hands of the one I loved.

And in a blazing light of tortuous comprehension, I was back in the room.

I closed my eyes, letting the horror of my memories wash over me, rivers of molten lava burning away the last remnants of my humanity. The emptiness that consumed my body left me barren and numb. All those years, all those years of living with him, loving him, doing everything in my power to seduce him, and all the time he knew, he knew that he had killed me.

I wanted to scream and rip the world apart. I wanted... I wanted my pain to end.

A gentle finger brushed the side of my cheek and I knew he was back. I could smell him, that slight sulphurous odour that clung to his magnificence.

"So you know," said Melek gently, with a voice both silky and seductive.

"Yes." I could not look at him. I could not stand to look at his beautiful face, not while my head overflowed with such ugliness. A finger curled through my hair. I wanted to snap it off his hand and feed it to that stunning face.

"You always suspected, really, didn't you?"

"Yes." The word split my lip with barbed anger.

"You loved him in life, and you needed to love him in death. You blocked out all that he did. You refused to believe he killed you so that in death you could continue to love him."

"Yes!" I flew at him with all my fury, my muscles straining with rage, and I glared into his dark magnificence with all the defiance I could muster. "Yes! What more do you want me to say? Tell me what you want me to say!"

Melek didn't flinch. His gaze burned into me, simmering with sympathy, boiling with love.

"Are you happy now? Do you want a piece of me, too?

Well, I'm sorry to disappoint, I have nothing left to give, the fucking vampire took it all."

"On the contrary, dear heart." The palm of his hand brushed my burning cheek. "You have found yourself."

I turned away from him, swooning at his touch. He overwhelmed me. Just the feel of him against my skin made my innards explode with desire—he made me feel things I knew were wrong, and I couldn't make up my mind if I gave a shit or not.

The screech of splitting metal made me look down. Long sharp talons lay embedded in the metal, tearing at the surface like paper, demon fingers, my fingers. I marvelled at the luminescence of my skin, my veins pulsing with energy. They were beautiful. I could feel my body willing the change, wanting to become, to give in to the desire that burned. Was I beautiful?

I was losing myself. I was spiralling out of control and I didn't give a fuck.

"Why are you here?" My words barely penetrated the gauze of devastation that engulfed me.

"Because you need me."

Something about his statement infuriated me. I was already on the edge, poised upon a precipice of pure desperation, and I needed to hurt something. The silver Death Head rings glinted on the table, the sight of them sickening, filling me with rage, and I scooped them up in my demon hand and threw them at the wall with a scream of pure unearthly rage that poured unfettered from my gut, shaking the foundations of the building to their roots. The rings collided with the brick like bullets, sending out fragments of chipped stone that flew in all directions.

His hand touched my back and I shivered involuntarily.

"Let it out, dear heart, don't hold back, not with me. Tell me how you feel."

"Angry." Why should I hold back? The thought hit me like an epiphany. Why shouldn't I burn down the world for what it had done, for what *he* had done to me? Why should the world go on while I did not? I would have that cunt's head in my hands, and I would send the world to Hell to do it. It could all crash and burn.

I spun around, grabbed Melek by the shoulders and pushed him backward, slamming him into the brick with such violence the brick shattered.

"Betrayed! I feel betrayed and used! I feel like a twat for trusting the wrong person, and I feel like I deserved everything I got for loving the wrong man. I am so angry, I am so full of rage I can feel it burning me from the inside, and I want to breathe fire across the world for what it has done!"

"Then why don't you do just that?" His words shocked me. There was so much sincerity in them and so much belief burning in his eyes, the absolute belief I could do it, an absolute belief in me.

My lips slammed into his and our tongues explored each other's mouths with alarming urgency. Teeth grated against teeth and we groped each other's body with bestial ferocity, flames leaping across my flesh wherever his fingers touched. I felt him transform beneath my touch, felt my own body complete its journey from a possessed host to raging demon. I had become more than a ghost, more than a bag of flesh and bone, and I liked it. We were two beasts thrusting against each other with a passion that burned from Hell itself.

"Tear down the world, dear heart, my beloved, my dark angel." His voice was so deep, so sibilant, and it sent a thrill of ecstasy surging through my body.

My body felt so powerful, my face, my arms, all of me glowing with a demonic energy that transformed my flesh. I had become the fallen one, I was Asmodeus, the great tempter of men, the burning scythe of Satan, I would smite all those who betrayed me and all those they held dear. I would burn down the world and make them understand the true depths of my despair.

Every movement felt new to me. My feet touched the floor so lightly, sending up wisps of smoke from beneath my cloven hooves. I wrapped my huge clawed hand around the face of the nearest corpse, I felt its skin bubble beneath my divine touch, and when I moved my hand away, I saw the outline of my hand branded into the blistered, dead flesh. A laugh, cruel and guttural, erupted from my chest, a new voice, a powerful voice. I was powerful.

"Am I not beautiful, my love?" He moved forward and ran a single claw down my front, my glowing flesh steaming at his touch, lower, until his hand rested upon my erection.

"You are the most beautiful thing I have ever seen." He went down on his knees, his gaze never leaving my own. Then he took my cock in his mouth. I gripped his shoulders with sharp unforgiving claws, drawing blood through his furry skin, making him gasp with pleasure. My head jerked back with a cry as I felt his forked tongue flicker across the head of my cock, the serpent coiling around my shaft to unfurl in one long measured stroke then he swallowed me deep, balls and all. The sensation of his wet throat surrounding my dick was more than I could stand and I came, pumping long and hard down his throat, screaming with each surge of my ejaculation as he gulped down every greedy mouthful.

I clamped his head between my hands and brought his lips to mine, covering his mouth, probing hungrily, devouring him like an animal, tasting myself upon his tongue.

"The Prince of Darkness is a gentleman."

He threw his horned head back and laughed. "King Lear. Act three, scene four. Shakespeare was quite the little devil, you know."

Gunfire, screaming, tearing through the night, I could hear the sound of dying, of men fighting for their pathetic lives, being torn limb from limb. I could smell their mounting fear, and I loved it.

"And so it begins." Melek grinned widely. "Go, dear heart, do your thing, be beautiful."

I gripped the edge of the table with one hand and flung it effortlessly across the room, sending metal and flesh crashing against the far wall in a shower of twisted limbs and steel. The power that burned through my veins felt magnificent. With the palm of my fantastic hand against the door, I pushed, and it tore away from its hinges and fell to the floor in a cloud of dust. I stood on the threshold, tentative, excited, and I looked back at that glorious being who nodded his encouragement as a parent to a child on their first day at school.

"Play nicely, dear heart."

I stepped out into a night filled with the sound of terror. The smell of it swelled my nostrils and I inhaled deeply, savouring its delicious tang, wallowing in its intoxicating aroma. It excited me, thrilled every inch of my flesh so that strummed in sympathy, as though every pore wanted to inhale its share of the fear that decorated the night. Death stalked Welwelsburg Castle—wait until they got a look at me.

Suddenly a soldier ran around the corner, rifle in both hands, a trembling bag of shit and piss. His fear turned to disbelief and terror as his bulging eyes fell upon my glowing form. I held out my big arms toward him to offer a loving embrace just as his jaw hit the floor.

"Come not between the dragon and his wrath!" I

proclaimed with a voice so deep and rich I barely recognised it. The world had suddenly become my stage, and my audience was death.

The tip of the rifle exploded with a flash of sparks, an ejaculate of powder and metal that hurtled toward me like a streaking comet. I could see the bullet careening toward me as though time itself slowed down, demonstrating an aerodynamic feat of incredible beauty as it sliced through the thin atmosphere with barely a hint of resistance, glowing hotly as a miniature sun. I marvelled as the projectile hit my chest and bounced away harmlessly, doing no more damage than a pea shot from a simple straw. What were bullets to me? What were humans to me, I who was demon?

In a movement too swift for him to comprehend, I reached out, grabbed his head and twisted. It came away from his shoulders in one satisfying crunch, stringy elastic gristle and bone snapping away as the body fell to the floor, twitching. I lifted the head and turned it around so I could look upon those dead eyes and I saw myself looking back at me.

I was stunning.

A sudden thought hit me as I stared at the head resting in the palm of my open hand. I felt it come over me with a delicious shiver and I held out my hand in the stance made famous by so many before me.

"Alas... no, I can't... I shouldn't." I giggled. But the temptation was already there, and who was I to deny temptation?

As I opened my mouth to continue, another soldier ran around the corner and nearly slammed into my hard body. My free hand lashed out and wrapped long fingers around his face, while simultaneously ramming him against the brick of the wall. His gun fell useless to the floor and his scream went unanswered into the palm of my hand. I leaned into him, my eyes burning into his terrified face.

"How rude. Do not interrupt me again!"

I straightened up, the head in the palm of one hand and the struggling soldier pressed against the wall in the other. I coughed to clear my throat and I assumed the position.

"Alas poor Yorick! I knew him, Horatio

"A fellow of infinite jest, of most excellent fancy

"He hath borne me on his back a thousand times

"And now, how abhorred on my imagination it is!

"My gorge rims at it."

I threw my head back and laughed with absolute abandonment. It felt so good. I looked at my captive, who was slowly turning blue, but his gaze never left my face.

"You know, I think old Shakespeare may have been a bit of a queer. I particularly love the rimming part don't you? No?" I offered the severed head to my captive, who was beginning to lose consciousness.

"Don't ever let it be said that I don't give head." I pressed his head into the brick, where it burst like a melon. Shattered bone and brain matter oozed between my fingers, and I let the dead thing fall limply to the floor before throwing the head away into the screaming night.

Screams of terror and pain rent through the darkness, so I headed toward them, eager to add my own brand of chaos to the proceedings.

But more than that, I wanted to find *him*.

A phoenix burning through the sky, I leaped with one stride onto a nearby roof, flying through the air with a grace that escaped me in life and defeated me in death. My new eyes and my new ears brought the night alive with light. I could see them running through the camp, flickers of burning life in hues of orange and red, scurrying aimlessly through the blackness in a vain attempt to stay alive. Someone had freed the prisoners, and below me, it was a melee of bodies as shots fired indiscriminately into the night. Bodies fell and bodies fled. A feast for my eyes, and I wanted to devour it.

My demonic eyes took in the watchtower looming over the camp, a huge silent sentinel rearing into the night. I leaped up into the wooden spider, only to find that someone had beaten me to it. A mangled body lay in a pool of blood inside the wooden box, a soldier, his throat ripped open and ragged, abandoned, left to bleed out across the floor to fill the small space with his own juice. It smelled delicious.

He had been there. I could smell him. His stench assaulted my nostrils and insulted my senses. But why would he waste so much blood? After all, had he not sucked me dry?

I looked out over the camp from my bloody perch, my nasal passages clogged with the stench of vampire. He was out there somewhere, there amongst the unknowing dead, his precious humans. Fucking hypocrite.

And then I saw it, in the far corner of the camp and I knew what I had to do. Before the idea had time to crystallise, I was leaping from roof to roof, bounding toward the compound with its boxes of treasure.

Two armed guards stood nervously at the gates, their guns twitching in their hands. Beyond them, I saw the boxes, silent gravestones in the waning moonlight, boxes that contained death, glorious, indiscriminate death.

I swooped down on the unsuspecting men, a burning angel before their terrified eyes. They lifted their guns, but I snatched them from their hands before their brains could tell their fingers to pull the triggers. They cowered against the chain link fence and I lifted the rifles, one in each hand and pointed the muzzles into their faces.

"Open your mouths." I placed the muzzles against their lips and started to push. "Open your mouths or I will push them through your frail flesh and shatter your teeth where you stand."

The one on the right tried to run. Bang! The rifle went off, but the bullet missed his face as he moved, slicing through his shoulder blade instead. With an agonising cry, he fell to the floor.

"Open your mouth," I said to the remaining soldier. He obeyed. I rammed the tip of the rifle between his teeth, feeling the grate of the metal against enamel, like fingernails against a chalkboard. I could smell the piss running down his legs.

"Watch." I raised my foot, brought it down onto the floored soldiers head and pushed, slowly, inexorably. Mud began to part around his face and suddenly his hands and his legs began to thrash against the sopping ground as mud oozed into his screaming mouth and into his terrified eyes. I pushed harder, forcing his head deep into the quagmire until there was barely anything left above the surface.

"As flies to wanton boys, are we to the gods

"They kill us for their sport."

Suddenly a loud crack split through the night as my foot crashed through his skull. At least his arms and legs stopped twitching. I stepped out of his head and looked at my remaining victim, pinned against the fence with the riffle in his mouth. He knew he was going to die. It wafted out of his every pore. I could taste it on my tongue.

"Have you ever sucked dick? No? Well, I'm going to teach you how to deep throat. Now just relax your muscles." I pushed the barrel in further. His hands clawed at the metal pathetically as he gagged.

"No, no, no, you are not doing it right. Relax. Open the back of your throat."

Bang! His head exploded in a glorious pattern through the fence and across the nearest boxes that shuddered as the blood hit them, the creatures inside excited by the smell of blood.

"Oops."

I threw the rifle aside and ripped the gates from their hinges. So many of them, all so hungry, all so desperate to be set free from their offending sigils. I would free them. I would set them free from their bonds to drain the life from every stinking human in that camp, to gorge themselves on all those lives that Eli held in such high regard. I would see the world consumed by the fangs of hunger, destroyed by the same insatiable thirst that consumed me.

So many boxes, my undead audience, so silent in their tombs, and I could feel their anticipation. The clouds parted from the moon, illuminating my brilliance in an arc of radiant light, and my stage was prepared.

"This is the excellent foppery of the world,

"That, when we are sick in fortune—often the surfeit of our own behaviours—

"We make guilty of our disasters the sun, the moon and the stars—

"As if we were villains by necessity—

"Fools by heavenly compulsion—

"Knaves, thieves and treachers,

"By spherical predominance—

"Drunkards, liars and adulterers,

"By an enforced obedience of planetary influence—

"And all that we are evil in,

"By divine thrusting on—

"An admiral evasion of whoremaster man,

"To lay his goatish disposition to the charge of a star!"

Chapter Twenty-three: Dead Camp Seven

As related by Eli

Time had no meaning as I sat there, staring into Joseph's dead face. Minutes, hours, days, I had no idea. But it was long enough for his body to stiffen in my hands, long enough for the poisonous cloud to settle on my shoulders, a dusting of early morning frost in a sea of sparkling dead.

I didn't even know him, not really. How could I? I had only just met him. But in that place so full of darkness he was a shining beacon, a ray of light illuminating that which had died within me, a flame to rekindle my faith in humanity. He was all that I was not, gentle, compassionate, human.

And I would show no compassion, no kindness. I would wipe the Nazi shits off the boot of Paderborn forest, and I would scrape deeply.

Metal ground against metal, tearing me away from the desolation of my shattered mind. I lay back into a sea of dead limbs, feeling the avalanche of bodies crushing down on me in a never-ending tidal wave of death and at the crest of that wave of bereavement lay Joseph, the pinnacle on my carapace of the dead.

I didn't need to breathe, but I was doing so, and heavily. It was my anger trying to vent itself from my body, trying to extinguish the flame of wrath that threatened to devour me, that threatened to devour the world. I could barely contain it.

The doors opened. I heard them crack against the external brickwork, and I could smell the night air rushing in to exhume the rank odour of death. My ears filled with the rustle of heavy-duty plastic and the ominous sound of laboured breathing, breathing filtered and re-filtered through thick protective masks.

Movement. The bodies quivered around me as unsteady feet picked their way through the carnage. A figure, I glimpsed it through the crack made by someone's armpit. Thick heavy-duty rubber clothing, a silhouette carved from the pages of a Jules Vern nightmare. Two great round eyes glistened through black glass while a long insectoid snout wound from the front of the face, down and around the back. He bent down, closer, the hiss of his breathing unit drowning out the sound of the fear banging against my temples.

Hands reached out and pulled the frail, broken body of Joseph away from me. They were touching him, lifting him without care, without respect. I let my rage coarse through my body as it propelled me out of that dead sea with a force that could shatter bone. I was a raging monster rising from the ashes of a broken people, my face a blazing tempest of vampiric majesty and my hands, two-razor sharp fiends that slashed outward without direction, without mercy.

There were two of them. And they didn't stand a chance. The first swing of my arms ripped the macabre mask from the face of the nearest, while the swing of my second hand ripped through plastic and flesh on the chest of the other. Blood, skin and rubber flew across a landscape of dusted corpses, but I did not linger to admire the beauty of scarlet against the white of cyanide.

The first rubber man gasped as his lungs absorbed the final dregs of the poison still present in the air. He covered his mouth and his nose with rubber-encased hands, but I pulled off his arms, flinging the bloody limbs across the room. He did not seem to care about the poison anymore because his mouth opened wide to accommodate the scream that issued forth and as he turned, he created a spiralling fountain of red as the blood pumped mercilessly from the stumps of his arms. Warm red stickiness exploded across my nakedness, but the blood of that fiend repulsed me, I would not drink it. Instead, I twisted his screaming head until it snapped and he crumpled to the floor.

Meanwhile, the second rubber man tried to crawl his way to the door, propelling himself across an uneven ground by one hand while the other tried desperately to hold his innards within his opened chest. I lifted into the air and came down with one leg either side of him. He turned over in terror, screaming through a mask barely clinging to his white face. My hands plunged down into the wound I had already made and pulled it open, ribs cracking and splintering beneath the onslaught of my pitiless fingers, spitting blood and pulp into my twisted face. I held up his heart for his dying eyes to see, but the life had already faded from them. At least his screaming stopped.

I stepped out into the night, a glistening, naked vision of white smeared with red gore, a twisted nightmare from the depths of Dante's mind. My body burned with anger, my fingers itching to rip heads from bodies and limbs from sockets. People were going to die, by my hand, and I would show no mercy.

I felt the bullet tear through my shoulder before I heard the bang. It entered through the top of my left shoulder and exited just below my left nipple. I felt no pain, just anger and an irritating itch as the wound began to heal. I looked up into the astounded face of a soldier, standing on the roof above me, his rifle trembling in his hands. He shouted something unintelligible to someone over his shoulder. I rose into the air so that when he looked back, my face was level with his, and the scream that belched from his mouth was music to my ears. I lunged forward, my teeth sinking roughly into the nape of his neck, and I clenched that tenuous skin between my lips and fangs as I continued to rise into the air. I could feel the strands of gristle and skin parting between my lips and as the soldier thrashed wildly in my mouth. The tear began to spread across his neck, blood falling in a warm red shower to the rooftop below.

A hail of bullets erupted from below to interrupt my flight of crimson. My ears rang to the sound of his hysterical screaming and I liked it. Blood rained down on him as he shot indiscriminately into the air, bullets blasting through my captive's arms, through my legs, through my stomach. But at last, the flesh between my teeth parted with a wet ripping explosion of blood and the body plummeted to the roof, landing on the head of the second soldier, who collapsed under its weight.

The soldier's limbs thrashed wildly beneath the corpse as I came to rest at his side. Eyes wide with dread blinked at me through a stream of blood. I skittered down behind his head and bent over so my eyes were above his. He lay suddenly still, whimpering, barely breathing. Slowly, very slowly, I opened my mouth, my fangs long and magnificent. Wider and wider, my mouth stretching until I felt my jaw crack and dislocate, but it continued to widen until my skin threatened to rip across my face. I brought my mouth down, slowly, my fangs sank into the soldier's eyes, my lower teeth clamping around the underside of his head, and I closed my mouth until his eyes exploded against my tongue and his skull cracked against my lower jaw. The body shuddered and convulsed with a last spasm of life, and then I released him, optical fluid, and brain matter dribbling down my chin.

I lifted my head and roared into the night, clenching my

fists at the heavens in such defiance as to bring down God himself. The stars glared at me, pulsing with disappointment, but I did not care. I did not care what God thought, what Daniyyel would think. Fuck the bloody lot of them. All I could taste was the metallic tang of fury on my lips and the desire to tear, to rip and to maim, to shatter the Nazi cunts that would snuff out the lives of so many innocents, and nothing else mattered.

Innocents, the concept chimed in my head to remind me of my path. I leaped from the rooftop to land in the cold mud, urgency coursing through my veins, my purpose so vivid and real. It would not be long before someone raised the alarm—I had little time left and Nazis to kill.

A bullet sang into the mud next to my foot. I swung around just in time to see a flash from one of the watchtowers as another bullet hurtled in my direction. I moved like the wind, flashing through the air with a graceful leap, reaching the tower in one swift blur of flight. I clung to the edge of the box as the soldier within desperately tried to focus his aim. Before he could level his rifle, I flipped into the tower, somersaulting as my talons lashed out to rip across the skin of his throat, severing his head from his body in one swift move.

Suddenly a blaze of white light hit me, illuminating the headless corpse as it spun on the spot, spraying blood. I looked into the harsh white light to see the searchlight bearing down on me from a second tower.

The noise started low and slow, building with a quickening intensity as the siren started. I leaped into the light, crossing the huge distance between towers in the blink of an eye, landing on the glass surface of the searchlight to the terrified scream of its operator. He staggered back in absolute terror. I grinned with satisfaction. I stood upright on the glass, the piercing white light illuminating me from below, the musculature of my body standing out in thick red blood, and I knew I was beautiful, a glowing vision of wrath.

The siren picked up speed, its haunting melody pulsing across the camp in a last desperate call to arms. The soldier, frantically turning the handle, could not tear his eyes away from me, and I wanted him, I wanted to feel him rip apart in my hands, and I wanted to see his blood varnish the floor. I leaped off the searchlight and landed at his feet, but before he could react, I ripped the handle off the siren and impaled him through the heart, blood exploding from his back as the metal spike erupted from his left shoulder blade. Before his dying eyes had time to focus on the metal sticking out of his chest, I swept up the second soldier and thrust his head into the spotlight, which exploded in a shower of sparks and blood, just as the body of the impaled soldier crumpled to the ground amid white-hot sparks that skittered across the wooden floor. And the floor glistened black with blood.

No more sirens. No more light. Fucking excellent.

Rows of huts lay beneath me. I somersaulted out of the tower and landed before a padlocked door that I ripped and tore from its hinges with ease. I bellowed into the dark interior.

"You are free!"

Ghostly faces emerged from the darkness, but I did not want them to see my monster, so I turned away, straight into a group of oncoming soldiers.

"Free the others," I shouted as I ran headlong into the advancing army. The prisoners were free, and I could do nothing more except give them a fighting chance.

The soldiers stopped in their tracks when they saw the bloodied naked fiend before them, a hissing storm of teeth and claws. Their hesitation was their downfall.

Everything happened in a blur. As my right foot landed in front of the first soldier, my left leg kicked out to hit the second, sending him flying with a hard crack into a brick wall. I lifted the first man off his feet, swung him around in a whirl of blinding speed, and let him fly into the group of remaining men who fell like skittles. I leaped onto a nearby roof just as a horde of screaming, furious prisoners charged into the fray, brandishing shovels, axes, crowbars, everyday items weaponised in the hands of a vengeful, angry mob. The prisoners were fighting back, and it made me smile.

I saw a figure fleeing through the maze of buildings to my left, a blur of black and white stripe. It was my Kapo.

I ran along the ridge of the roof with him fleeing just below, running as though the devil himself bit at his heels. I reached the apex of the roof and threw myself into the night, soaring through the darkness with nothing but the wind whistling against my body to make a sound. I landed in a tight crouch before the terrified Kapo, who fell backward onto the floor with a strangled yelp, and I unfurled before him, slowly, deliberately, like a precious flower greeting the sun, my arms stretching out as I stood, all in one beautifully smooth movement. The howl of panic that escaped from his lips sent a thrill of excitement coursing through my loins and I was hard.

"Not so fucking smart now are you?"

"Stay away from me... stay away from me, you fucking freak!" He scuttled backward, fear bubbling and frothing from his lips. I walked toward him slowly, inhaling the intense cloud of fright that drenched the space around him, tasting his adrenalin on my tongue. Fucking delicious.

"How many have died at your hands?"

"Not enough of you fucking freaks!" My hand flashed out and grabbed his arm. I twisted and pulled. The Kapo screamed in agony as bone and skin crunched and split and I felt the joint pop out of his shoulder. He felt it, too.

"Not so fucking chopsy now, are we?" The skin wound so

tightly around the joint that it split like a popped balloon and the Kapo howled into the night as I pulled the limb free, blood pumping from the wound. I brought the dripping stump up to my face and sniffed, my nose wrinkling with disgust.

"Your blood is so fucking rank not even I would drink it."

He writhed around on the floor, blood spurting across the muddy ground as he tried to stem the flow with his one good hand.

"Go to... hell... cock sucker."

There was just no helping some people.

I hunkered down and ripped his trousers from around his wriggling legs. A torrent of harsh language and filth punctuated his agonising screams as my sharp nails tore at his exposed flesh. I grabbed his ankles and flipped him over.

"You going to fuck my tight ass you filthy bastard?"

"I'm more of a bottom man myself. No, you're going to fuck yourself."

I shoved the limb where the sun did not shine. By the time I finished he resembled a fucking starfish, a mumbling, drooling, purple lipped Echinoderm.

I bent over his shuddering body and whispered into his dying ear. "How satisfying to know you can take more than a finger."

I left him like that, to die in a pool of his own shit and blood, his body a wrecked parody of all that he detested. It was a fitting end for someone who helped kill so many, and I did it without pleasure, without mercy and without remorse.

The sound of sporadic gunfire and screams filled my ears, so I flew to the rooftops once more. Hope had fanned the flames of renewed faith and turned the tide against the oppressors — the Nazis were losing.

And then a random head landed at my feet. For a

moment, I was too shocked to move, too shocked to think. What manner of monster, other than me, could do such a thing? But then it hit me and I was suddenly afraid, very afraid.

Don't let it be Mal, I kept telling myself, over and over, *don't let it be Mal.*

I scanned the area, perfect supernatural vision picking out every detail. I saw Jews mowed down by gunfire — I saw Nazi troops fighting for their lives, then I saw a huge glowing demon stomping toward the box enclosure, flesh transparent and pulsing with energy.

My heart broke. My knees buckled beneath me and I stumbled and fell from the roof, falling to the ground with a thump.

Not him, please not him.

Gunfire. Screaming. Terror.

That thing — that demon at the gates of the enclosure, so far removed from man, so far removed from him, not Mal, not my friend, my ghost and yet I had seen it in my dream, Mal, my best friend, giving in to the dark side.

Welwelsburg would break me yet.

Running, on my feet and running, a naked blood-smeared monster tearing through the night. My own fears ripped my vampire from my face and all my fury, all my anger fell away, evaporating in a haze of hopeless desperation to get to him, to reach him before it was too late, to pull him back into the light.

Mal could not go. Not like that.

I would not lose Mal. I could not lose Mal.

He was beautiful. Malachi stood amongst the boxes with open arms, tall and strong, so very self-assured. His body, sculptured to perfection, his transparent flesh glowing with a pulsing light that danced across the boxes, the elegance of his movements and the strength of his presence, all conspired to move me. He was breath-taking.

A magnificently clawed hand paused over a crucifix, poised to rip it from the surface of the nearest box.

My chest heaved, the sight of him filling me with such sadness.

"Malachi?" My voice was but a tremulous whisper upon my lips. The beast froze then slowly, oh so very slowly, he turned to face me.

His eyes — my god, his eyes were so yellow, two suns, burning with life. A forked tongue slithered between sharp teeth, tasting the air between us. And he knew I was afraid — the crooked smile that creased his face told me so. Then his voice, the voice of a demon, so deep and so sibilant and yet unmistakably his, Malachi's, echoed in my ears, and I wanted to weep.

"You are not worth the dust which the rude wind blows in your face!"

And then he charged.

I offered no resistance. I wanted to take whatever he threw at me. I deserved it. I closed my eyes in anticipation of pain, wanting it to hurt, wanting to feel something other than the misery that gnawed at my bones. But the blow never came.

I opened my eyes and he was standing before me, his yellow-eyed gaze piercing my flesh. I did not flinch. I gave no outward sign of the terror and anguish that flushed through my bowels.

"Let me look into the eyes of he who has betrayed me so heinously." His hot, putrid breath brushed against my skin making my skin crawl.

He knew. My bowels fell out of my ass and my world spiralled out of control, my shame blossoming across my face for all to see.

"You know, then."

"Yes." He stepped back, his eyes devouring me. "I know."

"How? Did Melek tell you?"

"Does it matter? What matters is I did not hear it from you."

"I'm sorry, I'm so sorry, please let me explain, let me tell you what happened."

"No!" The earth shook and the wind howled at his words. "You do not get to say those words to me, vampire! You have nothing to say that matters to me... but you can say it to him."

The demons body convulsed violently, features and limbs folding in on themselves in an avalanche of burning, liquid flesh. Then he stood before me, Malachi, not the ghost, but Malachi the man, in all his human vulnerability, as he had that fateful night in London.

"Mal!" I was so pleased to see him, my friend and companion. The man I killed. His head was down and I could not see his face, his camp, innocent, childish face.

"Mal?"

When he looked up, I wanted the ground to open up and burn me. Tears poured down his flushed cheeks from eyes red with pain, and his face betrayed such deep sadness that his grief took form in my heart, a shard of ice cutting through my very being.

"I loved you so much." Each letter of each word dripped with pain as they tumbled from his trembling mouth. "I thought you to be the most beautiful thing that I have ever seen. All I ever wanted was to love you, even if you could not love me back... and I continued to love you even in death, even in ignorance. How could you do that to me?"

"But I did love you, I still do..."

"But not enough! I was never enough was I? I pulled you from the edge of oblivion, nursed you through your pain. But what about my pain? All the time you knew, and you let me love you, you let me care for you. You let me die!"

He fell to his knees, great heavy sobs tearing at his wretched body. Before I knew what I was doing, I was at his side, my arms wrapped around his grief stricken body.

"How could I tell you, Mal? I was going to tell you, I wanted to tell you, but I could never find the words. I could never find the courage, then time went on and on and the longer I left it the harder it became. I was a coward. I am a coward." I rocked his shivering body in my arms, his head against my chest, his hot living tears pouring down my blood soaked torso.

"But you killed me. I gave you my love, and you killed me."

His terrible, agony-laced words were killing me.

"You don't know what I went through, what he did to me." I was crying too, I could not help it. "Gideon destroyed me, I loved him so much, so very much, he was my world and he threw it back in my face. He crushed me, Mal, he left me, I was so alone, so afraid. I was less than I am now, less than the man you helped me to become. And I can't expect you to understand that..."

"But I do understand that—you did it to me! I loved you, so very, very much and you threw my love back in my face!"

"No, Mal, no, you may think that you loved me, but you didn't, you couldn't, your loves are so fleeting, so temporary, how can you possibly understand a love that spans generations, a love that should have lasted until the sun burned out of the sky! You couldn't know, you couldn't."

"All love burns, Eli. All love is consuming. It is what we do with it which matters, not the time it encompasses."

"I was so angry that night. I was so hurt, so distraught, I could not see straight, or think straight. She threw me out of London, and it was the last straw. I broke. It could have been anyone that night, anyone."

"But it was my soul you took, my soul. It was not yours to take! I would have given it to you gladly, to be immortal by your side, companion, friend, lover. That I would have given gladly. But what I am, a spirit, a mere memory of that which I was, unable to feel, unable to touch the thing that I still love so much... you have given me an eternity of purgatory, an eternity of nothing. Do I deserve that?"

His words sliced through my flesh with utter precision, and the pain of them reached every square inch of my body. I felt the old despair rear its dark head, the need, the desire to end my existence, to free the world of my eternal suffering. The pain spiralled around me in a whirling vortex of darkness, and my eyes went black as my sight left me in a moment of all-consuming panic.

I closed my eyes and let our sorrow wash over us, two lost souls weeping into the mud, broken beyond recognition and I did not know how to put us back together. Did I deserve to mend? All that I loved, all that I touched, ruined, destroyed by my own selfish desires. Malachi, his life ended by my own bitter hands. Damnation was calling my name, and I deserved it.

"I'm sorry, Malachi. I'm so sorry, forgive me, please forgive me."

"No!" The word exploded from his lips like a sonic boom as Malachi ripped himself away from my arms, once more the shimmering demon. "I will never forgive you!"

The pain hit me in the side of my chest and my ribs shattered as his cloven foot slammed into it. I flew through the air horizontal to the ground, and my back slammed painfully into a wall, my spine shattering.

"The weight of this sad time we must obey

"Speak what we feel, not what we ought to say.

"The oldest hath borne most —

"We that are young shall never see so much,

"Nor live so long."

He turned away from my shattered body toward the enclosure. I could not understand why he would turn away, why he would not tear me limb from limb when he could do so, so easily. I wanted him to rip me apart, to make me suffer, to cause me unendurable pain, but he turned away, discarded me. And then I saw with disbelieving eyes what he was doing. He reached the nearest box and ripped the sealing Sigel from its front before moving onto the next.

"Mal, Mal, no, you don't know what you're doing! For the love of God, Mal no!"

"Not for the love of God, Eli, not for the love of *him!*"

The lid of the box heaved and creaked as nails wiggled free. Grey fingers forced their way through the gap, gripped the edge of the lid and pushed, loosening it further.

"You don't know what you are doing," I pleaded, dragging my broken body toward the enclosure. My spine cracked and shifted beneath my skin as it tried to heal, but I had to ignore the pain, crawl through my agony, because I had to stop him, I had to make him understand.

"They will destroy everything in their path. If you let them out, they will kill everything in this camp. Everyone."

"And that, my dear heart, is my intention! Let them tear apart those foolish humans you care about so very much. Let them do what they do best, just as you did, let them feed! Let them butcher! Let the night burn with rivers of blood!"

"But they won't hurt me. They can't hurt me, and that's what you really want isn't it, to hurt me?"

He paused as he ripped the fifth protective Sigel from its place. I shuddered as his yellow eyes focussed upon me, and I realised I had lost him. Mal, my Mal, was gone, replaced by a demon, consumed by anger and vengeance. And I felt utterly lost.

"But it will hurt you." So much satisfaction thrummed

through his voice, so much amusement on his face, so much malice in his eyes. It felt like that moment in Buckingham Palace when I knew Gideon was lost to me, that I would never see him again. It felt like he had died, except there was no funeral, no period of mourning, just never-ending grief eating away at me. And that was how it felt as I stared into the demon's triumphant face—I was watching Malachi die, for the second time. And it was my fault. For the second time it was my fault.

But the demon was right. It would hurt me. To see innocents die because of my actions would tear me apart, for as long as I lived, for all of eternity, the guilt, the torment of spilt blood, of never-ending death, of a slaughter that I caused. I would live forever in the darkness of my own shame.

A group of them emerged from the boxes, four ferals, with a fifth beginning to crawl from another box. Their flesh glowed, a dull putrid grey in the moonlight, the skin of their faces stretched tight against animalistic skulls, sharp needle teeth protruding from between hungry, grey lips. They huddled together in a tight group, their arms held in front of their chests, long fingers dripping downward. And their numbers grew. Six ferals stood swaying in the moonlight.

Festooned on their backs, with tentacles wrapped around their throats, sat the Quellor Demons. The ferals' eyes remained black as the Quellor slept, dormant. and my only hope was that they would remain that way. If the Quellor awoke, the feral would be unstoppable.

I closed my eyes and tried to compel them. I was Menarche, I should have been able to bend them to my will, but no matter how hard I tried, I could not connect— something pushed me back, repelling my command. I felt the dull yellow eyes of the Quellor Demons flicker in my direction and I knew it was useless. Even dormant, their hold on the feral was absolute.

The demon chuckled cruelly. "How does it feel to be so helpless?"

Eight ferals, nine, ten — Welwelsburg would drown in its own blood.

Satisfied with his little army, the demon stalked to the front of the vampires, who cowered away from his terrible gaze.

"Do not fear me, my pretties." His voice was a veritable purr, and he opened his arms wide as if to embrace them. "You are all my children now!"

He looked at me then, his face alive with glee. "Fasten your seatbelts — it's going to be a bumpy night." Then he addressed the ferals, his voice rising to a high-pitched cry that shattered the night. "Fly, my pretties! Fly!"

They scurried out of the enclosure, their gangly joints cracking as they moved. One of the ferals skittered over to my prone figure and hunkered down to get a better look at me, sniffing the air around my face. A flaccid wet tongue flashed out from between salivating lips and brushed against my cheek and the creature hissed, recognising its brethren before scurrying away to join the others, leaping lithely across the rooftops.

My spine snapped back into shape as I heaved myself off the ground. I looked at the disappearing monsters and the demon that glowed in the enclosure, torn between my friend and humanity. Someone screamed in the distance, but the sound was cut ominously, short and the horror of it glued me to the spot. Was that a Nazi or a prisoner? The feral would not discriminate.

I ran blindly into the night. As I raced around a building, I came across a group of soldiers fighting off two ferals, and they were losing in a catastrophic melee of blood and fangs. I told myself they didn't matter, that they had it coming, and

I ignored them, told myself they were not fit to be a part of the human race, and I kept on running, their dying, terrified screams fucking me in the back.

The sounds of torture filled my head, so much relentless screaming, so much of it I could not tell where it was coming from. Never had I felt so helpless. I stopped running, turning on the spot, confused, desperate. I felt people dying everywhere, so much dying, so much blood, blood that stained my hands, my fault — it was all my fault.

"Hello, Eli." The voice of an angel. I spun around, shocked to see Daniyyel standing before me.

"What the fuck are you doing here? I don't have time for your bullshit." The sight of him inflamed my anger, I needed help, not divine guidance.

"I am here to help."

Fuck me, I didn't see that coming. But I didn't have time to argue. "About bloody time. Look, there's a bunch of feral on the loose, Malachi has gone all demon on me, and there's something going on in the castle. They have arrived, Dan, the Mother and Father, they are here."

"Yes. I know." Quell fucking surprise. "But I have come to offer you a choice."

"For fucks sake, Dan, what is it with you and choices?" I did nothing to temper the frustration in my voice. People were dying, and he was standing in front of me procrastinating. "Why are you just standing there moving your lips? Why aren't you doing something?"

"Do not piss in my face, vampire! Listen!"

I bowed my head in supplication, but I was gagging to plant my fist in his mouth. "I should not be here, and I risk much by doing so. I am offering you my help, but understand that if I do this now I can never do so again."

"Always a fucking catch with you. Go on."

"I told you, Eli, there is an agreement between Heaven

and Hell, a Covenant that cannot be broken. We do not get involved. If I help you now — and you must consider that point very carefully — if I help you now, then that will entitle the other side to interfere as well. So make your choice. Do you want my help now? Or would you rather keep that card to play later?"

"Now, I need your help now!" I tried not to sound so desperate, but I failed.

"I can save your prisoners for you. I can take Isaiah back to his son. I could destroy Hitler. Or I could rip the demon out of Malachi. One shot, Eli, what will it be?"

Why did I have to choose just one? Why could I not have all those things? Why couldn't he just help?

Malachi, he could help Malachi, he could save him.

"Can you help Mal? Can you bring him back?" I was not sure, but I thought I detected the briefest hint of a smile cross his lips, just a flicker. It was hard to tell with an angel.

"Yes."

"Save him. Please, Daniyyel, please." The tears came fast and furious, streaming down my cheeks. "Please save Malachi for me... just... bring him back for me." There was no other choice — I owed Mal, I owed him more, but if I could just give him that much, if I could just save him that once, then I could deal with the rest.

He nodded once, a subtle bow of the head. "Turn around, Eli." I did as he said. Blinding white light suddenly blazed around me, and even though I shut my eyes as tight as I could, the light still burned through my eyeballs. I felt a gust of wind against my back that rose above my head, crushing me in its downdraft, and then he was gone.

Renewed hope surged through my veins. If that one obstacle, if that one impossible problem could be solved by one impossible solution, then I could save the prisoners. I would not allow another innocent to die that night. If Mal could be saved, if my friend could be brought back, then I could do that much.

Screaming hit me from all directions and I closed my eyes, visualising the sound, homing in on its vibrations. I focussed, concentrated, my vampire blooming across my skin and I felt it, guiding me inexorably toward the sound, and I knew the direction, I could smell the fear as I lifted into the sky, the itching on my back between my shoulder blades carrying me into the brisk night air toward Hell.

Cold icy wind battered my skin as I flew high above the camp, turning slowly in the air, aiming my senses through the fury of nature. The heavens opened to empty heavy shards of ice and rain upon my body, almost as though someone above was trying to push me back onto the ground. But I was having none of it. I pushed my eyes to see through the wall of sleet that threatened to slice my flesh to ribbons, concentrating for all I was worth.

And then I saw them. The cruel pallid ferals stalking their prey, some on the ground crawling, some creeping across the rooftops, driving their helpless prey toward the gates. But the gates remained locked, freedom tantalisingly close as the monsters, hissing and snarling, crept closer, herding them into a dead end, so many helpless people clawing and hammering against the locked metal gates while a line of prisoners, carrying makeshift weapons, flanked their backs against the approaching vampires.

The ferals were close, and I could almost taste their anticipation, their desire for blood. I felt my own blood lust rise, heightening the adrenalin rush already pumping furiously through my veins. Two ferals leaped from the rooftops, the ones on the ground poised to strike. I shot out of the sky, landing in a fountain of slushy mud between the monsters and the prisoners.

I pulled the first monster out of the air before it could

land and swung it around with all my might, throwing it into the waterlogged night. I ripped a metal bar from the hands of a startled prisoner and began to slash and hack at every inch of grey flesh that wriggled before me, bits of bloodless matter and grey rotting gore flying through the air—I did not stop and I did not hesitate. My body was a blur in the darkness, a merciless spinning top of death, cutting a swath of devastation through the creatures that were my kin, and I cried with pain as they broke beneath my pitiless fingers.

Something landed on my back. Wild, clawed hands and feet dug into my skin, ripping and tearing, teeth piercing my throat. I screamed in shock, the pain burning through my body as the feral flayed me on the spot, sucking greedily at my neck.

I reached back with my right hand and dug my sharp fingers into its eyes. I felt the wet gelatinous globes pop beneath my nails, but I pushed my fingers in deeper until they felt skull. Then I pulled and twisted. Its weak dead skull cracked and I felt its teeth withdraw from my bleeding neck. With every ounce of strength left in my rapidly weakening body, I pulled my hand forward, ripping the feral's head off its rotting shoulders, the body falling limp from my back. I flung the head at another advancing vampire, sending the beast sprawling backward into the mud with a screeching howl.

Without hesitation, I dived headlong into the panicked crowd. Humans scattered in all directions, fleeing from me, terrified of my monstrous appearance, and I could not blame them. I grabbed the padlocks and twisted the metal in my hands, screaming into the hard sheet of rain and ice that pummelled me from above, my veins bulging in my arms and neck with the exertion, but there was nothing left, my strength gone, my body spent, and I knew it. If I couldn't get those gates open, the prisoners would die and I barely had enough strength left to stand on my own two feet. I needed to feed and I needed to heal.

I let go of the metal, leaning against the gates, my lungs sucking in great heavy gulps of cold air, trying to shock my body into working, but my muscles were weak and my body defeated, useless. My eyes stung with tears, my voice a tortured howl of desperation and anger. I had to save them. I had to.

A metal bar pushed its way into my fingers, the old man's hands trembling as he passed it to me. So old, so frail, a bag of skin and bone in wet sodden rags. But he looked at me with such hope, such desperate hope. I tried to say thank you, but my teeth, longer than usual because of my hunger, lacerated my lower lip and his face, his beautiful sad face said he was terrified, yet he didn't flinch, laying instead a gentle, encouraging hand upon my shoulder. And I loved him for that.

I jammed the bar into the lock and I twisted. My mouth opened wide in a silent howl of pain as my shoulders and arms strained against the defiant metal, but suddenly, with a loud satisfying snap, the lock fell from the gates.

"Run! Run and don't stop!" With a cheer of triumph, the crowd surged forward and the gates swung mercifully open. As they ran past me, the tears flowed freely down my cheeks, tears of relief and happiness as they ran from Welwelsburg Camp. They were free, and it was the best feeling in the world.

As the bodies thinned out around me, I turned to face the advancing army of feral vampires, their black eyes beacons of hatred blazing through the rain. Four remained. One I had beheaded with my own bare hands, three lay in unrecognisable lumps of broken limbs and rotting flesh and two had metal spikes impaling their twisted bodies. But as I watched, the remains started to move before my unbelieving eyes. Mangled bodies pulled themselves together — withered hands wrenched metal from pierced chests, the head I had thrown into the night squiggled across the floor, propelling itself forward on strands of vein and bloody cord. Through the whole nightmare scene, I saw flailing tentacles pull and reassemble body parts with lightning speed until the fallen beasts stood on their feet once more, the Quellor Demons pulsing obscenely on their backs.

Ten feral vampires stood before me, ten feral vampires with demons on their backs. And I could not kill them.

I had nothing left, I felt desperately weak, dizzy with hunger, my body broken in so many places that I knew they could easily rip me apart. Would I die? I didn't know. I had never been torn limb from limb before. Would I lie there in a pile of twitching limbs trying to pull myself together again? Or would I crumble into a mote of merciful dust?

There was an old saying in London, in for a penny, in for a pound.

"Right, you grey skinned twats, who's first?"

They hurtled toward me, a wall of black eyes and teeth. I closed my eyes, wishing it to be over, safe in the knowledge the prisoners were free, knowing Mal was free and hoping that oblivion would come quickly. But for the second time that night, nothing happened. I tentatively opened my eyes. The ferals stood directly before me, inches from my flesh, hands raised in preparation for the strike, their pallid lips peeled back from needle sharp teeth.

Their eyes glowed red, blazing out of their skulls with a terrifying intelligence and I realised the Quellor Demons were awake. They sat on the ferals' backs, lumps of pulsating malignancy with yellow eyes that held me in their malicious gaze, and I wished at that moment they had torn me apart, because the alternative was too horrifying to contemplate. The ferals had red eyes, controlled by the yellow-eyed demons on their backs, which meant they were here.

"I would like to see you try, just for the hell of it. Go on, give it a go, make me laugh, but I fear it would just be a waste of my valuable time," said The Father, gloating from behind them. She stood next to him, stroking his chest with her long unfinished fingers.

"Oh what a shame, my sweet, I was so looking forward to seeing him in little pieces."

I heaved, bile spilling from my mouth and splattering across my blood-drenched skin. The sound of their voices filled me with terror, consumed me with cold dread, a hopelessness that drowned my empty heart with despair. To stand there, before their cruel eyes once again, was more than I could stomach.

"Besides, my sweet, now we have two of them for our little Jew to play with."

"Oh how marvellous. Better send the children home, then."

"Yes, my dear, that would seem like the prudent thing to do at this point, wouldn't you say?"

The Mother swayed gently, the Quellor Demons pulsing and throbbing in unison to her movements. Pale yellow eyes flickered with recognition and slowly, the red-eyed feral turned.

Blackness crept across my vision. My body was failing, and they had found me. I stumbled, my legs weak as the last vestiges of my strength ebbed out of my limbs, so I let the darkness swallow me in its unfathomable depths, unable to fight against it, unwilling to try.

As the world converged into one tiny pinprick of light, my brain fired up with one final thought.

Two of them, he said two of them.

Chapter Twenty-four: The Black Vatican.

Heat, intense, searing against my cheek, snapped me awake with a start of panic. Flames so close they nearly singed the flesh off my face. My stomach heaved with bile. I was strapped tightly to a chair by coils of vicious barbed wire that bit into my skin with bloody efficiency, trapped, too weak to free myself and too lost to care. Nothing but flames before my blurred eyes, a threatening flicker accompanied by a chuckling sound that drifted to my ears through my terrified stupor.

"Himmler, darling, it would not do to damage the goods before our tests now would it?"

The flames withdrew and I could see the hand that held the torch, the large silver Death Head ring glinting with silver malevolence upon a stubby finger. A face, slightly round, hovered before my eyes, a look of frustration creasing his petulant features, and his grey-blue eyes burned with a deep-set intelligence behind a gleaming set of pince-nez. He had a small well-groomed moustache set above thin, colourless lips, a pale, sweaty complexion and jet-black hair that lay plastered to his scalp adding to his bovine appearance. But what really disturbed me was his smile. There was something contemptuous about it, something despicable curling at the comers of his lips.

"Just having a little sport, Mother," he said in a surprisingly well-educated voice, almost scholastic in quality. "I meant nothing by it. See, he is awake now."

He stepped to the side so I could better appreciate the

view, and my eyes widened as they took in the cavernous space that imprisoned me. The chamber was huge, circular by design, with a high domed ceiling made out of brick—it bore an uncanny resemblance to a beehive. In the centre of the domed ceiling sat a massive swastika carved out of stone, surrounded by a complex series of circles and intricate lines. Enormous flaming torches set into the curved walls cast immense shadows across the ceiling, and it looked for a moment as though the emblem moved and pulsated like some great writhing squid.

Around the circular room, glistening in black SS leather, sat twelve members of the Thule society, perched on crude stone seats, but they were insignificant compared to the two figures sitting languidly across their intricately carved thrones, the Mother and Father, their long fingers dripping down the skull-shaped armrests.

In the centre of the chamber roared a circular fire pit. Hot, orange-red flames danced so high they almost brushed the swastika above. Windows with very deep reveals punctuated the incredibly thick walls at intermittent intervals, and I got the impression, by the way of the deeply slanted windows, that the bulk of the chamber lay underground. It was a chamber of darkness, its walls steeped with dread and malice, an inner sanctum for the Thule society and its Vril leaders.

Directly opposite me, at the far end of the chamber, sat the extraordinary clockwork contraption with the huge block of ice sitting in its centre, and the ice was melting. The heat emanating from the pit had already made a fine job of dissolving much of its outer core, and I could clearly see a human figure encased within. And still it pulled my eyes toward it, commanding my attention. It wanted me to know it.

Two of them, he said two of them. Those words kept

firing through my brain. What did he mean—two of what, two of me? My stomach heaved and twisted in gut churning waves of nausea. I felt a fear creep over me unlike anything I had experienced before, it was so real, so tangible that it pricked at my skin with daggers of fathomless anxiety.

"Do you know where you are, vampire?"

I glared into his pig-like eyes, my mouth a tight slit of defiance. His hand flashed out across my cheek and my head snapped back violently.

"When I speak to you, it is customary that you open your lips and reply. Do I make myself quite clear, or shall I pluck those pretty eyes out of your head with my fingers, so we may converse by brail?" He leaned in close, his face utterly cold and his breath heavy with the smell of expensive tobacco. "Now, I shall ask again, do you know where you are?"

I forced my lips to part, barely spitting out one word. "No."

"Good! You are in the bowels of Welwelsburg Castle, my black basilica. I rebuilt this place from the foundation up—I spared no expense to realise my masterpiece. From here we will rule over the entire Nazi Empire, from here our Black Messiah will reach out to every corner of the earth to expand that empire. We are its beating spiritual heart and we are its ruling brain, we are the centre of the world. Welcome to the Black Vatican." He bowed—he actually bowed, like some pompous showman waiting for his standing ovation. Well, he would have a long fucking wait.

"You like the word black don't you? Do you think if you say it enough, it will make you more evil?"

His face exploded into a vicious snarl and he raised his clenched, ring-filled fist ready to strike. It was going to hurt.

"Himmler! You have had your fun, now come to Mother and be a good boy."

Himmler, suddenly sheepish, took his seat next to the Mother, and she stroked his knee affectionately. He positively rippled with pleasure at her touch. Suddenly The Father was standing before me, sneering down at me, his piercing yellow eyes seeing straight into my empty heart.

"Even the sight of you makes me want to vomit." Then he threw up, a thick putrid stream of unspeakable filth splashing across my body and across my face. Glutinous, unrecognisable lumps slid down my flesh and across my tightly clenched lips. The smell of bile stung my nostrils and burned my eyes.

"That's better," he declared, wiping his salivating mouth as the Mother giggled from behind a clenched fist. "Strange how you should be here now, at this time, in this place. You have an annoying habit of appearing where you are least wanted. But every cloud has a silver lining, don't you think? While your being here is an affront to my eyes, it is also quite serendipitous." He spun around and waved a long finger at a guard standing by a tall set of wooden doors. "Bring him in."

The doors opened and an SS officer wheeled in a metal trolley. An array of ornate objects littered the metal surface and I realised with horror I had seen them before, fakes and copies pretending to be the real thing, the Spear of Destiny, the weapon used to pierce the side of Christ by Gaius Cassius Longinus during the crucifixion. They were all so similar, hammered iron artefacts encased by decorations of shimmering gold. Some had an inner cavity filled with items bound in leather, items said to pertain to Christ and the one true cross, quite beautiful in their own way. To me they represented a past that had almost destroyed me, a past that caused me pain beyond endurance. And there they were again, laid out before me like a recurring nightmare.

Isaiah Silberman followed and he held, clutched to his

chest, another spear. It was bigger than the other artefacts and more ornate. He was reluctant to part with it when an SS officer held out a velvet cushion toward him, but a gun aimed directly at his head persuaded him otherwise.

"How touching, Isaiah. You have a particular fondness for that one, do you not? The Hapsburg Spear? The one our Dark Messiah first gazed upon when he met you all those many years ago."

Isaiah stiffened and his face wrought a glare of defiance. He had been proud once. "If you know so much, why do you need me here? You have the spears—I kept my part of the bargain. You promised to reunite me with my son."

My heart sighed at his words. If only he knew, if only I could tell him how close he was to Ethan. I had infiltrated Welwelsburg Castle in order to save him, and yet we both remained captives to our own dark pasts. How far we had both fallen.

"Ah, but your work is not over yet, my friend. You may have found all those relics claiming to be the true spear, but you have yet to verify which one, if any, is authentic. Have you not?" Isaiah's silence made The Father smile, a cruel twisted thing. "I thought as much. The deal was that you bring us the one true spear, and then—well, and then we shall see."

The Father reached out a long spidery hand, picked up one of the spears and turned it in his hand.

"It does not burn me—I feel nothing, just another fake, do you think? Let us see, shall we?" With astonishing swiftness, he plunged the spear into my side. Agony radiated through my body, my back arched in pain, the barbed wire cutting deeper into my flesh, shredding my skin.

"For the love of god what are you doing?" Isaiah pleaded, clearly shocked. To him I looked just like any other prisoner, just another man, beaten and bloody.

"Oh I'm sorry, didn't I tell you? Meet Eli, he's another Menarche. Now you have two to play with." He pulled the spear out of my side and tossed it into the flaming pit. As the metal withdrew from my ripped and torn flesh, I screamed, and what little blood I had left in my system trickled down my bound legs.

But even through my agony, his words registered with startling clarity. Two of them, another Menarche. Now you have two to play with. But it couldn't be, please God no, it couldn't be.

"Well, that one was obviously a fake, or the killer of my child here would be reduced to a jabbering fool. Oh, I'm sorry, did that hurt? Tough shit."

Isaiah looked horrified as the spear hissed and bubbled in the flames, the iron and gold already blistering in the intense heat. As The Father reached for another blade, the Mother slithered to his side and gently pulled his hands away from the sharp treats.

"Now my dear, no more, you know He will want to be present for this." She reached up and pulled his face toward her obscene lips, and tongues flickered eagerly between them, but Isaiah was staring at me in shock, recognition flickering across his face. He knew me. He knew who I was.

"As always, you are correct, my beloved. And when He arrives, he will honour our bargain, we shall be a family again."

My head exploded. I could not think straight. The block of rapidly melting ice beckoned to me, tormented me and I almost fooled myself into believing I recognised the form inside. But it couldn't be, not him, anything but him.

And what did they mean by family? *We shall be family again.* It was not possible.

Hysteria pulsed through my veins in unrelenting waves of crushing horror. Madness snapped at the last tenuous threads of my sanity. I flexed my arms against the barbed wire of my restraints until the flesh ripped from my bones, anything to keep me grounded in that mind fuck of a reality.

"Shall we call him, then?" The Mother was positively giddy with excitement.

"Yes, my dear, go do your thing."

The Father strolled back to his throne as the Mother sashayed over to an eager looking Himmler. She nodded to the sweating man, who leaped from his seat with eagerness, undoing his belt with shaky hands. The Father sat back in his throne and undid his trousers, slapping his own thick grey monster across his lap, black veined and throbbing, while she stood between his legs and pulled up her skirts, revealing her own vile nakedness. She bent over and took The Father's cock in her greedy mouth. Himmler moved around her, his own cock stiff in his hands as he pushed his dick inside the Mother's groin, gripping her roughly by the hips, the three of them moaning in obscene ecstasy. I had to look away for fear of vomiting.

Isaiah turned from the obscene show, his fists clenched tightly against his chest. I knew what was going through his mind — I saw the shame of it engraved into every line of his old face, the memory of his own violation by Hitler. I wanted to pull him close to me and tell him that his son was near, that I was going to release him from all the horror and depravity so readily flaunted before our offended eyes, but I was as powerless as he. Two mislaid souls trapped in despair surrounded by writhing demons. We were in Hell.

The sound of raw, painful sex reached a sickening crescendo just as the ground beneath our feet trembled. A huge bestial claw erupted from the fire pit, reached up into the ceiling, then crashed down onto the floor with a loud groaning boom that I felt in my bones. A second hand screamed from the fire, clutching at the air with fierce claws before both limbs heaved something massive from the pit—a huge set of twisted horns, a set of burning malevolent eyes, brighter than the fire that birthed them. A piercing roar issued from a frothing maw filled with glistening teeth, smothering the cavern with a foul stench that made me wretch. Then the body heaved itself out of the inferno and a massive set of leathery black wings unfurled, laced with pulsing veins, fanning the conflagration into a white-hot seething maelstrom of fury as the beast stepped out of the pit, its massive cloven feet grinding the flagstones to dust beneath it.

The thing from my dream raised itself above our heads in all its terrible majesty, a creature so huge as to dwarf the world. I knew the monster. I knew what he was. I knew who he was. The first of the fallen, the original demon, Melek, the devil, and he liked to make an entrance.

Poor Isaiah knelt on the floor at my feet with his hands covering his eyes, unable to look upon the thing that had manifested itself before his mortal eyes. The rotten stench overpowered him and he gagged uncontrollably, long thick strands of yellow bile dripping from his quivering lips to the floor.

"Oh how I do love a bit of gratuitous degeneracy to whet my appetite!" roared the beast.

Bone and fur diminished and liquefied. Wings shrivelled and claws withered as the monster melted away with a wet sticky implosion of energy that sucked the air out of the cavern and made our ears pop. And then there was just Melek, standing next to Isaiah, immaculate in his black suit and shiny spats. He laid a beautiful hand on the old man's shoulder, his soft velvety voice floating out of his perfectly formed, voluptuous lips.

"Do not be afraid of me, little man, you have done me a great service, I am most grateful."

Isaiah's body froze as Melek's words sank in. He hadn't known. All those years, serving the Mother and Father and he hadn't known, had no idea he was working for the devil. He dared to look up at Melek, his tired old face a rictus of utter disbelief and shock. My heart broke for him.

"I have done *you* a service?" he stammered, barely able to force the words out from between his lips.

"Why yes, dear heart. You have been hunting the spear for *me*, did you not know? How else am I to kill God?"

Isaiah paled visibly and he swayed where he knelt, and I thought for one heart-stopping moment he was going to pass out. His hands landed heavily on the stone floor with a loud slap as his body sagged forward, the final truth, the final burden too much for him to comprehend. Tears streamed down his cheeks.

"Kill God?"

"The spear is drenched with the blood of his son. When this war claims the lives of his most beloved creations, his beloved humans, and he deigns to leave his throne in Heaven and descend to the earth, I will be waiting for him. I will sink the blade that bears the blood of his son into his hypocritical heart and smite him from existence. So yes, dear heart, I am going to kill God." He delivered his lines with the calm certainty of a lunatic, every word spoken with an edge of deadly madness, and poor Isaiah looked distraught.

"I seem to remember you trying something like that before. How did that turn out for you?" I spoke up, trying to deflect his attention away from the old man.

For the first time, Melek's insane gaze fell upon my bound body. I felt the full weight of its wrath burrow into my flesh, blackness seeping in to corrupt my soul, and I squirmed beneath the yellow stare of his eyes, but they were nothing compared to the snarl that ripped across his face. With effortless grace, he leaped over to my bound body, his slavering lips dribbling across my torn skin, each drop of saliva burning into my tortured flesh like acid.

I should have withered to dust beneath his terrible fury. To see something so beautiful contorted with such blistering anger was a sight no eyes should ever witness.

"Don't you fucking dare mock me, you piece of worthless shit!" His hand lashed out across my face in a blur of stars and blackness. "You took my dear heart away from me."

"Excuse me if I can't quite form the words, but I seem to have a fist in my mouth. And there's a strange ringing in my ears, so forgive me if I ask you to repeat your question..." Sarcasm. Got to love it.

Melek roared with anger, his mouth tearing his face in half. Perhaps the ringing in my ears bit was a little too much after all.

"Malachi, you took Malachi from me! He was mine to claim, mine to love, what did you ever do for him other than rip his life away?"

"I beg your pardon? Run that by me again. You love Malachi?" I had not heard correctly, or they were all high on drugs, because that was the most fucked up thing I had ever heard.

But it did tell me one thing. Mal was free of the demon. Daniyyel had kept his word. Relief flushed through my fevered mind and tears hung heavy upon my eyes. Mal was safe.

"I don't know how you pulled him back, but you had no right."

"Oh, sorry, are you still talking?" A second slap ripped across my still burning cheek.

"I felt his dark beauty die in my heart—he was mine to love, and you tore him away from me. When I find out how you did it, I will rip your fucking head off your fucking shoulders, you spoiled little cunt. What do you know of love anyway? You couldn't keep that last one, could you? You're nothing but a cast-off, always have been, always will be."

Anger and fury suddenly burned through me, hot and tempestuous.

"You know nothing! You know nothing of Gideon, nothing, do you hear me!"

He leaned in. I could smell the sulphur oozing through his pores, his blazing hatred of the world hitting me with wave upon wave of nauseating loathing.

"I know more than you think, shit-head, you were not the only one he loved." He moved away as the horror of his words filtered through my shattered body, my broken mind trying desperately to understand his meaning, to comprehend another lie.

The Mother and Father flittered over to Melek's side and they took it in turn to kiss him, on the lips, with tongue. I wondered if Malachi, amongst others, had kissed those foul lips and I found it hurt me, pain crashing down on pain.

"Speaking of loved ones, we have brought him here, our beloved, so please, please do it now, you promised." A black tear spilled down the Mother's cheek.

Melek's terrible gaze did not leave my face as a smug grin rippled across his sadistic features, and suddenly I was afraid, terribly, terribly afraid.

"I will do it, just to piss this one off! Bring him in."

Two soldiers carried in the stretcher and laid it to rest before the thrones, the twisted form beneath obscured by the green brocade shroud. Another soldier carried in the golden cauldron and placed it upon a stone dais between the thrones. I felt sick. The mound on that stretcher wanted me, it wanted me to know it, and it wanted me to be afraid. It frightened me. The sight of it filled me with dread, a dread I had not felt in a very long time, familiar, all encompassing. I wanted to run from that world of demons, from that world of secrets and lies and pain, so much pain and so many fucking lies. Reality lay as shattered before my feet as my sanity.

Melek's eyes glittered at the sight of the beautiful golden vessel nestled between the thrones.

"Exquisitely crafted, moulded from the teeth of so many of those who have died in this interminable war. It's so good to recycle, do you not think?"

I kept my mouth shut. I had seen first-hand how people died at Welwelsburg. What had happened to those people, the corruption of their remains, was abhorrent to me. And that thing, glittering on its stone stand, crafted from the remains of so many dead, was an affront to life. It was an affront to God.

"And in death it shall bring life." Melek smirked.

The Father looked at me then, hatred transforming his inhuman countenance into one of pure loathing. He lashed out with an angry hand and ripped away the cloth from the stretcher to reveal a body. It was as dry and as withered as a leaf. Its long limbs lay crooked, its dry lips peeling back from a sunken face that still bore the scream of his death. But no matter how wizened the body had become in the years since his death, I still recognised it, still recognised the evil that poured from its parched flesh. It was Morbius, the Mother's and Father's child, born of pure evil, Morbius who died by my hand in London.

I saw the slick look of satisfaction explode across Melek's sly features, but I could pay him no heed. My eyes were transfixed on that desiccated corpse, the *thing* that had cost me so much, lying there, mocking me from beyond the grave and suddenly the cavernous space around me became so small. There were just the two of us, locked together in eternal hatred, eternal war. Eternal evil.

Pure hatred lay on that stretcher, pure monstrous evil I

thought I had killed. He was the blackest being to have ever walked the earth, a creature of remorseless cruelty I knew I had killed. Morbius, they were going to bring back Morbius, and in that moment, strapped to that chair bleeding and in pain, I had never felt so alone. All was lost. I was lost.

The Father leaned over the dried out thing and pulled something out of its chest. He gasped with pain as he held the tiny object in the palm of his hand, his huge eyes flashing wildly as something unseen burned through his mind and he nearly collapsed, but with a wail of defiance, he got to his feet and moved toward me, his whole body trembling with barely contained rage.

"Yes, vampire, look at him. Look upon the face of our beloved son, the son that *you* saw fit to destroy. Did you think you could eliminate a Menarche with nothing but a mere speck of wood? A splinter?"

The Father stood over me, the tiny splinter clasped between two long fingers, then he slowly, oh so very slowly pushed it into the skin of my stomach. The pain that ripped through my body was unbearable, filling my head with images, burning into my mind with terrifying clarity. They nearly burned me. I saw the nails as they drove into *his* hands, I saw and felt the nails driving into *his* ankles and I felt the agony and the despair of *his* dying, the loneliness, the bitter disappointment, the feeling of betrayal by those *he* loved. *His* despair was so total that it nearly consumed me and I screamed until no more sound could escape from my mouth.

Isaiah rushed forward and pulled the splinter out of my side, and the images vanished instantly. The pain became a dull throb that ebbed through my bowels and shot down my legs in waves of numbing electricity.

"Stop this madness!"

The Father looked outraged. He lifted a long arm to strike

the old man down, but Melek stopped his hand in mid-flight. For a moment, The Father looked as though he were going to retaliate as undisguised anger rippled across his face. The Mother rushed over and took him into her arms, pulling his head into her bosom as he began to weep, black tears pouring down his cheeks as wretched sobs shook his body.

"Forgive me, it has been so long, and every day without him has been an agony of suffering. Please, we have done what you asked, we have brought upon the world your Black Messiah, we have waged a war that is even now burning the world. We have made you an army of creatures to feed on the infidel race that He put on this earth to usurp our rightful place. We were not failures! He made us this way. He made us immortal. Is that our fault? No. So I am begging you, to be one more day without our son by our side is more torment than we can endure."

Melek brushed a gentle finger across The Father's cheek, wiping away a black tear.

"Then you shall endure no more, my friend. Put him in the fire."

With tremendous effort, The Father collected himself and with the Mother holding his hand, they went back to the stretcher then threw it into the pit, where the hungry flames consumed the body greedily. Suddenly the fire exploded with a tremendous *whump*, erupting into a fierce sapphire blue that transformed the cavern into a world of icy flickering light. A fierce hurricane raged around the fire pit forming a glowing vortex of bursting stars and blue flame, a column that reached toward the ceiling to embrace the swastika emblazoned upon the centre of the dome.

Noxious fumes, sulphur, burning flesh, permeated the air with its heavy, sickly odour, and a high-pitched screeching ripped through the storm and tore at my flesh, threatening to pull me into the fiery whirlpool of impenetrable light. Isaiah threw himself upon my body, as much to hold me in place as to save himself, and he screamed in my ear, his voice loud and hoarse, trying desperately to make himself heard above the terrible din.

"Hold on! Just look at me and hold on!" I looked into the face of that human, and what I saw there shamed my own bludgeoning terror. I saw no fear, just grim determination, and I saw for the first time the brave man from the diaries. He was not afraid to die and he was not afraid to put himself before others to save them, as he was saving me. He was a human, just a man, an Exorcist and a Vampire Slayer, shielding me from the raging inferno that threatened to suck us both into its fiery embrace.

The skin of my right arm tore from my bones as my arm sprang free of the barbed wire encasing it. Blood flew across my flapping skin, sucked into the spiralling vortex, consumed by the blue flames of the swirling nightmare. I felt my body begin to lift, the restraints weakening, my body tearing, but worse still, I could feel Isaiah slipping from me as the howling wind reached out to claim him. With what little strength I had left, I fought against the sucking vortex and wrapped my badly injured arm around Isaiah's back, pulling him hard against me, screaming with pain and terror.

Suddenly the howling wind died, and with a tremendous rush of energy, the burning vortex collapsed in on itself with a crushing *whoosh,* then silence. All that remained in the fire pit was a pile of smoking ashes.

"Thank you." Isaiah saw my arm and he blanched. "You're hurt..."

"Do not concern yourself about that, old man. We have other things to worry about."

The Mother and Father carried the golden cauldron and

placed it on the edge of the pit. To my astonishment, they climbed into the smouldering cinders and began to scoop handfuls of ash into the golden vessel. They worked with intense urgency, a silent desperation that in anyone else, I might have pitied. But I felt nothing but loathing and hatred for them. They had unleashed Morbius on the world once, and they were about to breathe life into the nightmare again.

With the vessel filled, they moved away, glancing at Melek with pitiful, beseeching faces. Melek indicated for them to go back to their thrones and they obeyed, their desperate gaze never leaving him. Melek picked up the cauldron and walked over to the block of melting ice, placing it beneath the tap that protruded from the front. He turned the tap, and a steady trickle of red flowed into the ash-filled receptacle.

"The blood of the first, still with the essence of *he* who died on the cross flowing through his veins. Just a spark, the faintest memory, that is all that is needed." He turned the tap off, and the blood ceased to flow.

I was more confused than ever. The monolith had taunted me since I first saw it and I thought I knew what it contained, a growing suspicion, a gnawing dread, but Melek's words left me baffled, and he laughed at my perplexed expression.

"Still the fool, Eli, still the fool." The chamber erupted with laughter. They were laughing at me.

"What is in that ice is no laughing matter!" Isaiah was furious. "What you are doing, the power that you wield is not yours to give! And it is not his to give!" His finger stabbed angrily toward the emerging figure in the ice.

The silhouette inside the ice fucked me in the head. When I looked at it, I wanted to cry, it filled me with such a profound sadness, an old feeling, old emotions I wanted to forget. My gut, my instincts, the old memories of pain, of despair, told me what was in that ice, but Melek's words confounded my reason, and nothing made sense.

"You know don't you, you feel it, but you don't want to believe it, you don't understand. Priceless." Melek walked around the pit and placed the cauldron before the Mother and Father. He rolled up his sleeve, extended his arm over the cauldron and using a long sharp fingernail, he ripped open his flesh, allowing his blood to pour into the vessel to mix with the concoction inside. The potion began to boil and bubble.

"Why don't you tell him, Isaiah, go on. Tell Eli what we have in there. See if he finally understands."

"No."

"Why? Feeling a bit guilty are we, dear heart, because trapping him in ice was your idea?" The cauldron was almost overflowing, its surface bubbling and hissing violently. "An inspired idea I must say — to trap him in ice. To think that you could trap such a thing in a moment of frozen time, when he has lived longer than any human that has walked this earth. Tell him. Tell him!"

Isaiah bowed his head in defeat, his voice barely a whisper. "Gaius Cassius Longinus. In the ice, it's Gaius Cassius Longinus."

The sentence ripped through my brain like a red-hot poker stuck up my ass, the words searing their meaning inside me. I could barely believe it—I who had fought the devil, I who had spoken with angels and demons. I could not conceive of such a thing.

"No, that's not possible, the man who created the Spear of Destiny, the guy who stabbed Christ on the cross? How... how can that be?"

"And the rest Isaiah, tell him the rest," gloated Melek, as though that particular revelation was not enough to blow anyone's mind.

At that moment, the Mother and Father leaped from their thrones screaming with excitement. The cauldron was glowing, the gold emanating a strange black light that pulsed with a dull throb, the sound of it reverberating through the floor. Thick viscous tendrils rose out of its surface, coiling in the space above, then twisting back in on themselves, plunging into the glowing miasma.

Suddenly the cauldron began to shudder. Then it moved, sliding across the floor until, with a resounding clang, it slammed into the side of the stone pit and toppled over, spilling thick black membranous gloop that slithered and throbbed across the cavern floor. Things coiled and bubbled upon its glutinous surface, glimpses of half formed organs and body parts that moved independently of each other.

Fascinated, the Mother and Father moved forward, staring transfixed into the viscous puddle that seemed to be growing steadily in volume, spreading across the floor until it was almost at their feet. With a bloodcurdling screech that ripped through my soul, a column of membranous fluid shot into the air, a quivering pilaster of gore that pulsed in time to the black heart beating at its centre. Wet writhing tubes connected the thing to the bloody puddle on the floor, pumping the lumpy liquid upward into the column that began to fill out, gradually coalescing into a humanoid shape. Two lidless eyes, fiercely green, slide out from a ripple of red-black slime, eyes that scanned its surroundings, eyes that saw me, a gaze that did not leave me. Twisted bone and hard defined musculature slithered over the coalescing corpse, locking body parts and organs into place, followed by pale opalescent skin that slid upward from the floor, knitting itself across muscle and sinew until a fully formed figure stood in a pool of glistening blood.

He raised his newly formed hands to his perfectly formed face, long, elegant, perfect fingers exploring his newly fashioned features. Those same hands pressed themselves against a graceful neck, veined with firm hard muscle and then slid down his body, feeling the curves and the definition of his perfect frame, the beautifully formed chest, the hard ripple of a well-defined stomach, the long thick member that hung twitching between long, strong legs.

Morbius had always been a stunner. Unlike his unearthly parents, he could just about pass as human, though no human had ever been so beautiful. His startling green eyes stood out from a face that said it wanted to fuck you and fuck you hard. Long black hair curled seductively around his broad masculine shoulders, and he had lips that you could kiss forever. Next to me, he was one of the most beautiful creatures I had ever seen. And I hated him. I hated him more than I hated anything else in the world. He tried to destroy the world once. He succeeded in destroying me.

He took my Gideon away.

And he was standing before me. My eyes saw him but my brain refused to believe it. He was dead—I killed him. I had purged the earth of his obscene presence. And yet, there he was, offending my eyes, darkening my spirit, back from the grave to ruin my life. I wanted to weep for the world, but most of all, I wanted to weep for myself.

His head swivelled on top of his shoulders, a sinewy movement that sent shivers down my spine. Morbius' powerful green eyes flickered across the astounded figures of his parents, who could only gaze upon their resurrected son in awe.

"Hello Mother, Father." My god, that voice. I had prayed never to hear it again. So rich in tone, so lyrical in deliverance. Smooth bastard. Then his head swivelled in my direction, cold eyes fixed on me, turning my blood to ice as he slithered in my direction.

I looked into his eyes, hopelessly lost in their pure

emerald beauty as he leaned in, smelling me. His lips parted, his tongue moistening his big plump lips. Then he kissed me, full on, with tongue. I resisted, but he pushed his tongue inside my mouth, feeling the sharpness of my teeth as they shot out from their sheaths in protest. He pulled away and he giggled.

"It was not so very long ago you welcomed my advances, Eli. Has that much really changed between you and me?"

"Why aren't you dead, you stinking son of a bitch?"

Morbius probed his chest as the briefest flash of confusion flickered across his face, then looked over to his parents questioningly.

"Where is it?" All eyes fell on Isaiah. Morbius moved in one fluid movement to stand before the defiant man and held out his hand. "Nice try, old man." Reluctantly, Isaiah reached into his pocket and pulled out the tiny splinter, placing it into Morbius' outstretched hand.

Morbius shuddered as the power of the splinter coursed through his system. Long black lashes fluttered and his flesh trembled as powerful images surged through his dark heart.

"Amazing, isn't it," he groaned through orgasmic lips, "what power such a little prick can possess. But a splinter? I don't think so. But fair play, you nearly had me, but you didn't reach my heart, Eli, the splinter did not reach my heart. If it had, well, then it might have been a very different story."

"But your body, I saw you crumble, I saw you destroyed, I saw it!" I felt my anger and my frustration hang on every word, and I hated myself for giving into it, but that thing had always brought out the worst in me.

"Ah, well there lies the nub of our little story, does it not. Does he know, Mother?"

"Yes, my child, but not all of it."

"Oh how wonderful! I do like surprises. Mother, Father,

may I?" His Menarche parents nodded their approval and he danced with glee. "Watch, you're going to like this, not a lot, but you will." He bounded over to the ice, his hands flashing with maniacal speed across the various levers and valves built into the mechanisms base. And he sang. He actually sang, his voice rising and falling in great melodious booms. Wagner's Ring Cycle, the fucker even made that sound good.

Great jets of broiling steam encompassed the ice, shooting hot and fierce from tubes spaced around its base. Within seconds, a hot curtain of steam concealed the monolith, screaming like a fox howling in the night. Morbius danced naked around the cacophony of noise and vapour, his arms gesticulating wildly as though he were conducting some invisible orchestra, his voice fighting against the sound of hissing steam and cracking ice. Large chunks of ice erupted from the curtain of hot vapour, crashing to the floor in great exploding pieces, a glittering shower of diamonds.

Suddenly, in a blur of movement, Morbius was standing over me, hands tracing the contours of my muscular chest.

"Exciting isn't it? Are you excited? Oh I'm *so* excited!" Then he was back in front of the disintegrating ice. With a final roaring rush of steam, the jets died away and the vapour began to dissipate.

I could see a vague shadow through the dying remnants of cloud that clung stubbornly to the shape. As the tenuous whispers of steam lifted its teasing veil, I could see a figure strapped to a chair, a tube embedded in his chest.

Then I saw his face.

"Eli, may I present Gaius Cassius Longinus."

My entire world fell out of my asshole. I wanted to run away and scream—I wanted to tear out my eyes and rip out my bleeding heart.

"What's the matter, Eli, no witty comebacks, no smart

remarks?"

Something inside me snapped. Nothing felt real, it was all a dream, all some terrible nightmare, because what I was looking at could not be real.

And then Morbius was back in my face, his huge green eyes gloating with triumph.

"Who do you see, Eli, go on, who do you see?"

Insurmountable pain—for so many years I had hidden it, buried it in the deepest darkest recesses of my pitch-black soul. The hurt, the memory of it, the feel of it. The agony of loss. I was so afraid of it. It had turned me into a killer once. It all came back to me then, as I looked at that figure strapped to that chair, pounding through my veins, hopeless despair and unending pain.

"It's not him... it can't be him..." The words tumbled out of my mouth in unintelligible whispers that ripped at my throat and gouged out my lips.

"Tell me who you see!" he screamed into my face.

"No!"

"Tell me who you see!"

And I broke.

"Gideon! I see Gideon!"

Gideon—I saw his face, and I did not want to believe it. I wanted to tear my eyes out from my head and burn them. I loved him, then he took that love away from me, leaving me with nothing but grief, alone in a chasm of despair that sucked me down into a landslide of self-destruction.

"He never told you, did he? Who he really is? So many secrets, so many lies. Secrets and lies, Eli, secrets and lies. My how they eat away at your soul, at anything that was once good and true. How I love them."

Gideon's head, for I could not think of him as Longinus, shifted and his eyes fluttered open. I saw their blueness from where I sat and my chest heaved within my body as his gaze fell upon me. Gideon saw me. My skin prickled and I felt my tears trickle down my face as my eyes betrayed me yet again. I had wasted so many tears over that man, and they poured from me yet again, wasted pearls of emotion that burned my flesh and crippled my spirit.

I could not read his expression. He had always been so painfully efficient at hiding his feelings. As I looked into that unfathomable face, I realised it was lying to me yet again — it had always been lying to me, because Gideon was not real. Gideon was a lie. His life with me was a lie.

How much more of me was there left to break?

"So, picture this," continued Morbius gaily, "there I was, legs in the air with this magnificent lump of Roman history, banging away at my ass with his great big cock, when low and behold he rips open a vein and allows me to feed."

Morbius looked at me then, wide-eyed and beautiful, deadly. Every word that escaped from his perfectly formed lips crucified me.

"Did he fuck you? No? Did he let you drink from him? No? What a shame. And what interesting blood it is, too." He shot the Mother and Father a dark look that would have withered most mortals. "I should have burned, after all, the blood of that Messianic fool is so concentrated in his veins, the blood of Christ compels you and all that shit, but guess what, I didn't burn, did I? No! Oh but I saw, I saw it all. You never knew, did you, how he became vampire, how he became Menarche? Well Gideon, or should I call you Gaius? You bad, bad boy, you. When he stabbed Christ with that spear, he ingested his blood. That's how he became a vampire, the first vampire. The blood of Christ transforms you!"

He laughed at his own joke, mad rippling peals of insanity that made me shiver.

"See what I did then? Yes? No? Never mind. So, where

was I? Ah yes, Gideon was fucking me and I was sucking his blood and just as it got interesting, you burst in, all jealousy and outrage, brandishing that pathetic splinter, that tiny piece of the true cross. So I slit Gideon's throat. It was the least I could do. And then you, the hero, plunged that relic into my chest and I collapsed, crippled and useless. But I didn't die, did I, not really. I should have turned to dust, but no, my body withered, yet I remained alive inside that shrivelled construct, conscious, oh so fucking conscious of all around me. All those years, trapped in there, seeing everything, hearing everything, powerless to move, powerless to make my screams heard. I was alive!" he screamed, his anguished torment whirling around the cavern and all the time his blazing eyes never left their focus on his parents, eyes full of anger, eyes full of pain, eyes that screamed betrayal.

"Mother! Father! I did not die! Why do you think that is?"

Gideon's focus did not leave my face throughout this monologue. He just stared at me, unreadable, stoic, and all I wanted to do was hit him. I knew he had secrets — he never talked about his past, and the subject of his vampire origins was strictly taboo, so the truth, so bluntly revealed, killed me with every syllable.

"Morbius you fucking cunt, come over here and suck me off some more, I don't think you did it quite right last time." Gideon, so gruff, rough, with such an oh-so-manly voice. He always was a bit coarse, a bit rugged, but always so very butch. Gaius Cassius Longinus, a Roman legionnaire. Rough manliness personified.

But he didn't like to fuck though, did he, oh no, always a turn over, that one. Lucky if I got it up the ass once a year. And what the fuck did I have to do to get a blowjob?

Did he give Melek a blowjob?

"Ah, he speaks." Morbius skipped over to Gideon and

gripped his hair cruelly in one hand, pulling his head back roughly. Gideon snarled—it was a deep guttural sound all too familiar to me. It meant he liked it. Morbius ran his tongue over my ex-boyfriend's dried lips, then they were kissing, a long passionate embrace of lips and tongue, and I found myself looking away as I felt my fury rise into my cheeks. Jealousy was the last thing I expected, or wanted, to feel.

"That was a clever move on your part, Gideon," panted Morbius breathlessly, "ensnaring me in such a fashion, letting me drink your blood, showing me the truth. Did you think that would bring me over? Did you think I would repent? Ha! Well played." He looked at me then, eyes cold burrowing into my soul. "But I know who you are."

I felt sick. My stomach churned. Tears fell from my eyes, I felt weak, weak beneath his stare, weak beneath the truth blazing from behind his eyes, my truth. That truth threatening to infect me suddenly frightened me more than he ever could.

"Are you not the greatest monster of them all?"

My soul shattered at his words and I tried to shut them out, but they rang around my head in great swathes of despair that tore at my flesh more viciously than any blade.

"Enough, Morbius, enough." The earth trembled as Melek bellowed his command, and even Morbius cowered from his wrath.

"We felt you leave us, my beloved." The Mother's grief was evident across her striking features. "A little part of us died with you that day."

"And from that moment on we hunted Longinus to the ends of the earth. And we caught him, for you, for you, my son."

Morbius wandered over to his parents and a sly smile creased his beautiful face and I shuddered. I never thought to see that expression again, that look of calculating evil, the malice that underpinned his beauty. He wrapped an arm around each of them, nestling his head into their shoulders, grinding his bare flesh into their leather.

"Oh you dear people," he declared with exaggerated exuberance. The Mother and Father seemed delighted by his reaction and embraced him enthusiastically, but Morbius pulled away, a contemptuous sneer transforming his face. "You say you have done this all for me? You needed Gideon for your own agenda, not as a gift for me. You need him to ratify the spears validity, is that not so?"

The Mother and Father looked suddenly nervous and squirmed uncomfortably beneath Morbius' penetrating gaze. It amused me to see them so anxious, but it also frightened me, because they were frightened of him.

"But you brought me back, and I suppose I should be grateful for that."

Morbius wandered over to the trolley, his fingers brushing over the shiny objects.

And all the time Melek glared at Gideon. I knew that look all too well, because I had given it myself. It was the unforgiving stare of the dumped.

"So. Same old, same old. The spear, spear, spear, spear. They are beautiful. Do you know which one is real yet?"

"No, child," said the Mother with a face like a slapped ass. "We were about to test them."

"Oh goody." Morbius picked up a spear and with lightning speed, plunged it into The Father's side. Shock and pain exploded across the Menarche's face as he screamed, black blood gushing from the ragged wound as he crumpled to his knees, shrieking through clenched teeth.

"And that, my dear *Father*, is for lying to me. Do you think I would not find out? Do you think I would not know? Don't lie to me again. You won't like me when I'm angry."

"Morbius! How dare you..."

"No! How fucking dare *you*. You lied to me. You suspected he was Longinus all along, didn't you? You knew his blood would paralyse me, didn't you? And yet you allowed me, your son, to endure living death. And what if you were wrong? Then would the splinter kill me? Is that how you treat your son?"

"But... we knew we could... bring you back. Melek promised us." And still the black blood flowed.

"But we love you, my son, we have always loved you, look what we have done for you."

The words registered in my tortured mind, but they did not sink in. All I could see was the liar strapped to the chair. Nothing else mattered.

Fury pouring from every pore of his body, Morbius leaned over his Father and spat into his face. "Do you love me, Father? Or am I just a pawn in your everlasting war with Grandad? Eden, I hope it's fucking worth it." Without care and without mercy, he pulled the spear out of The Father's flesh. "Well," he growled, licking the blood off the iron head, "it seems that one is a dud."

"Well, quite the family reunion, but at the risk of sounding a bore, could we please get on with it, places to be, things to do and all that, dear heart."

Morbius swept up an armful of the weapons and dropped them at Gideon's feet. His finger skipped through the air over each implement and I could see him mumble the words silently to himself, *eeny, meeny, miny, moe.*

"Ah fuck it!" His hand snatched up a spear and with a wail of fury, he plunged it into Gideon's heart. Gideon's head thrashed violently as his flesh tore beneath the onslaught of metal, red blood pumping from the tear in his chest, agony howling from his lying lips.

"Is this the one, Longinus? Is it? Tell me!" Morbius pulled

out the spear, picked up another, plunging it into the gaping hole, levering the blade backward and forward until I could almost hear it grating against bone. "No, not that one? How about this one, then?" Another blade plunged deeper into his heart, thick red blood gushing furiously from the wound, his screams a torture of sound. I struggled against my bonds with my one free hand, but I was so damaged and numb I could hardly use my fingers. I thrashed in my seat, desperate for freedom, consumed by the overwhelming desire to rip Morbius apart.

"Which one is it? Which one is it?" Morbius exploded with uncontrollable rage, his hands lashing out across every bare inch of Gideon's skin, ripping and clawing, ravaging his weakened body.

"I won't tell you, I will never tell you. Go to hell, you fucking prick."

Morbius reared back, arms rigid, hands clenched into fists, every sinew bulging in his hard body as he screamed, his rage filling the brick chamber with deafening force. It was then that I glanced at the velvet pillow still resting by my side, and I saw that it was empty. I looked at Isaiah and he looked at me, his hand clamped protectively against the pocket of his worn coat.

Morbius swung around, his face twisted by madness. "Where is it," he mumbled as he pounced on the metal trolley. "Where is it?" With a triumphant cry, he found what he was looking for, holding up the splinter before his wide eyes, body trembling with effort. So much power held in that fragment of wood, blood steeped with power, steeped with history, held between his trembling fingers. He advanced on Gideon.

Terror froze my muscles. Darkness fell upon me, thick and oppressive, its cruel hand grating against the corners of my mind, demanding that I watch, demanding that I witness the unfolding horror before my terrified eyes. And I did not want to watch. I did not want to see the man I had loved for so very long crumble into dust before my distraught eyes, despite the lies, despite the infidelity. I did not think I could survive it.

Morbius' hand hovered over Gideon's chest, his fingers holding the delicate shard over his washboard stomach.

"I liked you, Longinus. I may call you Longinus? It is, after all, your real name. But if you don't tell me which one is the real deal, I will drive this fragment into your body and watch as it makes its way to your heart. Blood attracted to blood, slowly. And it will reach your heart, and I will watch you turn to dust. Is that what you want? Is that how you want Eli to remember you, a pile of crumbling dust? So tell me Longinus, do be a good chap, which one is the genuine spear?"

Those eyes, I always thought them so deep, fathomless pools of manly beauty that I could swim in for all eternity. I loved those eyes, their clarity, their colour, the smart wickedness that flickered behind them, and as I looked into those tortured pools, he met my gaze and I fell into those orbs that were so full of desperation, so full of hopelessness and to my astonishment, full of regret.

I wasn't ready to let him go. I didn't want to let him go.

His eyes widened, pain clouding their exquisite beauty, mouth slack in a silent, desperate cry as Morbius drove the splinter into his flesh.

"Deeper," moaned Morbius in ecstasy, "just a little deeper. Can you feel it? Can you feel it moving inside you, searching out your heart?"

I felt something moving at my bound hand and I was shocked to see an SS soldier unwinding the barbs from my shredded flesh. I made to protest, but he silenced me with an urgent finger.

"Get Isaiah out," he whispered then he winked.

"Mal?"

"Just get the fuck out, Eli." I was so stunned I could barely move. Shame trickled down my spine, shame that he would save me, shame that he would risk himself again for me. But the disgrace that blackened my soul was nothing compared to the joy I felt at seeing him once again.

A hand gripped Mal's shoulder and he spun around, straight into the arms of Melek.

"Have you come back to me, dear heart?" Melek spoke with a yearning I did not think possible from such a being. I was amazed to see such passion burning in his eyes, passion for Mal, for my friend, and in that split second as I tore my ruined body out of that chair I could only see them, their gazes locked into each other's, loving each other.

Suddenly the room erupted into chaos as dozens of screaming prisoners charged into the chamber, shovels and pickaxes raised above their heads. Metal flew indiscriminately, hacking, dismembering, blood and body parts flying through the air in a melee of gory retaliation. Someone grabbed me, shook me from my stunned stupor and I looked into the face of an old man, the old man who had helped me open the gates.

"Go, my friend, go now, take your friends, and leave this godforsaken place." With a cry of rage, he lifted a crowbar and disappeared into the throng of wrestling bodies.

I leaped across the fire pit and ripped the restraints away from Gideon's convulsing body. He was writhing in agony, his face soaked with blood, clutching his chest, eyes blazing in terror.

"It's in me. I can feel it moving."

I pulled him out of the chair and was about to lead him away from the raging battle when a pair of hands gripped my shoulders and flung me crashing to the wall.

Morbius stood over me, his face alive with hatred and furry. He held a spear in each hand, raised above my weakened body ready to strike.

"You will not take him from me! He is mine!" His cruel mouth opened impossibly wide as a terrible howl issued from between his lips. I brought my hands up to protect my face and close my eyes against the oncoming agony of my own immolation as suddenly a hot stream of black liquid splashed across my face and body. I opened my eyes. Morbius stood clasping his neck, blood gushing from a slash that nearly severed his head from his shoulders. He stumbled and fell to the side of me, sliding down the brick wall in a smear of blood.

Hands lifted me off the floor, and for a moment I was too shocked to realise that my saviour was Isaiah, brandishing the Hapsburg Spear in his bloodied hand.

"Take my arm, lean on me."

With Isaiah's assistance, I pulled myself off the floor, dazed, in shock, my eyes barely taking in the bloodbath that surrounded me. Thule members battled against ravaged prisoners, but the Thule were stronger, the Quellor Demons on their backs giving them superior strength and agility. Bodies lay mangled and shattered, bodies of prisoners, those I had helped to set free, those who had come back to save me.

"I've got to help them, they don't stand a chance, let me help." I stumbled and fell, so very weak, the chamber spinning around my head.

Malachi appeared at my side, Gideon leaning heavily against him.

"Get the fuck out, Eli — they are here because they wanted to be here. They wanted to help you, so don't piss it back in their faces. Get out! Now!" I don't think I had ever heard Malachi sound so butch.

We ran, Malachi supporting Gideon, and Isaiah half dragging, half carrying me. From behind, I heard the screams of the dying. I heard gunfire and the roar of demons. But we did not stop and we did not look back — we fled, leaving those good men to their fate, those good men who were dying to save me.

We burst through a large set of arched doors into the dawn. Never had fresh air tasted so good. We emerged into battle, prisoners fighting the scattered remains of the Nazi contingent. As we pushed through the bodies piled around us, my eyes saw the ground stained with dark pools of blood, Nazi blood. At the sight of our group, a cheer went up, and the remaining prisoners began to run, great swaths of emaciated people pouring out of the camp into the surrounding forest. Welwelsburg Camp lay in tatters, a ruined shell littered with the bodies of its would be oppressors.

I could feel Isaiah weakening, his breaths puffing between blue lips in great heaving gasps as we began to climb the hill away from the camp and I pulled him up the steep slope with every ounce of strength I had left. He would not fall, not when we were so close, not when so many had fallen to aid our escape. I would deliver him to Ethan. With every last remnant of energy left in my body I would deliver him to Ethan.

As the slope levelled out, we collapsed gratefully into the soft green grass, just as the morning sun broke the skyline in a blaze of triumphant glory. We lay there breathless, unable to speak, Isaiah's hand clutched tightly in my own, holding me tight. A finger of sunlight cracked through the black clouds and touched our skin, and for a moment, just for the briefest of seconds, it felt as though God smiled down on us.

"We can't stop here," snapped Malachi as he reached us, Gideon in tow.

"I have to rest... nothing left," I gasped.

"Are they following us?" Isaiah let go of my hand and looked around nervously.

"Not yet, but they will," grumbled Gideon, "they have our scent now and they won't let us go."

"I can't make it, I haven't fed, no strength left."

"Feed on me." Gideon thrust out his arm toward me. The shock that split my face made him chuckle, but it was a humourless sound. "It makes no difference now, feed on me."

Gideon had never allowed me to drink his blood, ever. He forbade it. So many arguments, so many bitter, hurtful arguments over his reluctance to share that intimate part of himself. He would drink of me freely during our lovemaking, tearing at my flesh, swallowing greedily, knowing everything about me with each gulp, a pleasure denied to me, his lover. And that denial killed a little part of me each time, rotted my heart until I could no longer ask, no longer beg, no longer care.

And there he was, holding out his arm toward me, giving me permission, telling me to drink.

My teeth extended, I gripped Gideon's arm in both hands and gently pierced his wrist, and as my teeth broke the flesh and I sucked in that first mouthful of blood, my mind exploded with everything that was Gideon. I saw Gaius Cassius Longinus, his life in Rome and his long painful transformation into the first vampire, and the terrible loneliness that followed. And there was more, so much more that flashed before my eyes, images that I could not understand, wave upon wave of emotion, of pain, of desperation and loneliness, always alone, never his true self, the desolation of an existence known only to him.

And then there was me. The truth of it hit me and I finally understood. I withdrew my teeth from his vein as my heart shattered within my ribcage bleeding out into my empty soul, and I could not believe it.

"You should have told me." I could barely speak, the pain tumbling from my face as I met his hard, unsympathetic gaze. "All this time and you didn't tell me. You knew. You knew it all. How could you do that to me?"

"Can you fly?" he demanded coldly as though I hadn't seen, as though I didn't know.

"Yes." I tore my gaze away from him, unwilling to show him the hurt that was turning me to ash more efficiently than any splinter.

"Then take Isaiah with you, I can make my own way back to Alte." So cold, so heartless and without as much as a second glance he sped off into the trees of Paderborn forest.

My head was in a spin. I stared into the pit of impending madness and it beckoned to me with open arms. I could not take any more. What remained of my sanity clung to my reason by tenuous threads and I closed my eyes, feeling his blood rushing through my veins, filling my head with all that terrible truth, and I wanted to scream.

"Eli?" Mal, there was still Mal. My faithful trusted friend. He was still standing before me, albeit in the body of another man, but at least he had come back for me, he had tried to help me, and he was still by my side.

The outline of the soldier blurred as the spirit of my friend ripped itself from the body, relinquishing its hold on his mortal flesh with a sickening snap of entwined souls. The soldier slumped to the ground, unconscious, leaving the shimmering outline of Malachi before my grateful eyes. He was still there—he had forgiven me, because he was still there.

"I'm not coming with you, Eli."

I heard the words but they did not register. I thought I had nothing else left to lose. But I was wrong, so fucking wrong.

"Don't look at me like that," he admonished. "I can't come back with you, not after everything that has happened. Not after what you have done—did to me."

"Are you going with Melek?" It was all I could think of to say. Of all the things I could have said, my mouth opened and those pathetic words fell out. My eyes stung and my heart ached, desperate to find the words, the words that would make him stay, the words that would make him forgive, the words that would make him stay my friend.

"Not that it is any business of yours, but no."

"Do you love him?" Curse my mouth.

"I do not know how I feel, and what does it matter to you if I did? You do not love me, do you?" Bitter accusation laced his tone, one that cut me to the bone. I wanted to tell him how much I cared, but my lips would not move—my lips were too ashamed to move.

His face darkened at my silence. "No, I thought not. How you can sit there in silence after what you did, I do not know. You might very well be ashamed, because I am ashamed of you."

My head jerked upward to look at him, tears, cold against my flesh, pouring down my face. There it was, the final thing stripped away from me, the respect of my best friend. I reached out to touch him but he backed away, and I felt my voice crash against my lips in a pitiful whimper.

"Do not touch me. I am leaving, there must be others out there like me, other *victims*." He emphasised the word, twisting the knife deeper into my bleeding heart. "I am going to find them and I am going to help them. They are alone and they are frightened, and I intend to do something about that."

"I'm sorry, Malachi, I'm so sorry." Pathetic words from the remains of a pathetic man.

"Go home, Eli, go back to Alte. Ethan is waiting for you and Gideon — at least you *can* love *them*."

Without another word, he turned his back on me and walked away, his outline fading as he took away his friendship, as he took away that last shred of humanity I had left to cling to, vanishing until there was nothing left of him but a whisper in the distance. And then he was gone.

"Ethan? My Ethan is here?" Isaiah looked so pale I thought he would collapse. But his face was so full of hope, of happiness that he dare not give life.

"Yes, he's here. That's why I came, because of Ethan, to bring you to him." They were words, just words, just a string of meaningless sounds that tumbled from my numb lips without care or without thought, because nothing mattered, not anymore.

The truth was there for me to see, indisputable — how would I be able to live with myself now that I knew, I, the greatest monster of them all.

Isaiah rushed toward me, his hands gripping my shoulders. "Take me to him. Please take me to my son."

I took the old man into my arms and I glanced back at Welwelsburg Camp for the last time. Fingers of tentative sunlight broke through the grey canopy of cloud to caress the castle, and to look upon its sun kissed majesty that terrible morning was to forget the true horror underlying its bricks and mortar. I wanted to reduce the area to ash, to wipe it clean from the face of the earth, to cleanse the valley of its all-prevailing evil. The entire edifice was but a scar on the surface of the planet. Scars never fade, and scars always remember the pain that caused them. I was walking proof of that.

I felt the sensation begin between my shoulder blades, the rippling and tickling of my skin as we rose into the air, two fragile, lost souls soaring above the clouds into a sky so blue and so clear and together we flew across the high green tips of Paderborn forest toward Alte, toward my home, toward Ethan.

I was flying toward Gideon, toward Gaius Cassius Longinus, the one who made me a vampire.

Epilogue

I was an angel. I was the right hand of God. With great power comes great responsibility. And I had flaunted that power, so I sat upon the Twin Mountains above the world created by my Father and I waited for him, my brother, so we could discuss terms.

I, Daniyyel, amongst the highest of the Seraphim, had broken the Covenant. I intervened—I ripped the gestating demon from Malachi's soul, thus depriving my opposite number of his prize and he would require recompense. It was our way.

The Twin Mountains had always been the place for such meetings. The two black granite fingers reached toward my Father's Heaven with effortless grace, their flat tops above the milky atmosphere of cloud that clung to earth in a protective dome. There the sky met the stars and the blurring of blue into stratospheric black radiated through every known colour of the spectrum and others yet un-named. My Father was truly a creator of astounding imagination and beauty, such a pity he was so desperately lost.

"I wonder sometimes Daniyyel, why we bother to go through such formalities."

Melek had sat on the opposite peak. He looked immaculate as always in his black suit, but I had to wonder at his taste in shoes.

"Because it is the civilised thing to do—to do otherwise would bring chaos and disorder, and while they may be

208

desirable bedfellows for you, they are not our way, dear brother, as well you know."

"Bedfellows! How uncharacteristically fruity of you."

"I have done a lot this day that is uncharacteristic of me."

"Yes, indeed. Why Malachi? You took him away from me. Why?" While his words held no malice, I was surprised to hear the underlying emotion that dusted them. It took a lot to surprise me.

"Because Eli wished it so."

"Because Eli wished it so. That creature would not know love if it fucked him up the ass!"

"Brother, please, do you mind?"

"Oh saints preserve us, Daniyyel, get a grip. Don't you ever crave a good shag? No, don't answer that, too much information. So why now, brother, why do you choose to break the Covenant now, you who have never committed a crime in all your long existence, and why for that spoiled little runt? These are compelling questions, brother, and I require satisfaction."

"It's his time. Eli and Ethan deserve their chance at last. You know this."

"I see. So what if I tell them first?"

"What?"

"I thought that would grab your attention."

"And you really think that would be enough to bring Father down? Well I have news for you — I think you will find that Eli already knows the truth."

"Some of it, brother, some of it. Ethan, however, does not. And he is the one that counts. That should piss Father off, don't you think?"

"You can't do that!" I tried to sound as shocked and as indignant as I could. Melek had to believe my sincerity. There was too much at stake.

"Oh, but I think I can. Yes! I can! You have broken the

Covenant, oh brother dearest, so therefore I am entitled to a little discretion in return, one intervention on my behalf to balance the scales. And that is what I choose."

It had worked, and Melek had taken the bait. Slowly, oh so slowly I got to my feet and spread my magnificent wings, sunlight and starlight glinting off their silvery strands in a blaze of refracted colour. Melek also stood, his black wings spreading across the sky in huge glistening waves of darkness. And he looked so very, very pleased with himself.

"Then we have nothing left to say to one another, brother."

"No, I guess we don't. Thank you for this, Daniyyel – I couldn't have fucked this up better myself!" With a gust of wind, he flew into the air, like a beautiful black eagle soaring through the heavens. He paused in mid-air, stretched his arms and wings in a pose made so famous in churches throughout the world, and even I could not help but smile at the audacity of the man. With a final flash of his pearly white teeth, he plummeted downward, the atmosphere parting before him with a flicker of dazzling light that rippled through the layers of cloud as it swallowed him from view.

I knew he would not be able to resist. As I climbed toward my Heaven, I did so not with a heavy heart, but perhaps an apprehensive one. I would record the meeting in the Book of Transgression, as was our way, but Father would not see it, Father would not realise the position I had so very cunningly manoeuvred him. His indifference toward the world he had created would be his undoing.

I had gambled everything with a dangerous strategy. And Heaven would either stand or fall by my hand.

About the Author

I think that as I approach that milestone that is fifty, I must be one of the oldest gamers on the face of this earth. Many a day you will find me lashed to my PS4 enjoying a good session of Skyrim. Who doesn't love a good session of Skyrim?

I love writing—I have done it since I was a child when I would happily write about the latest episode of Doctor Who (Tom Baker in those days) in my schoolbooks. Growing up and becoming a business owner with my friend Jayne left little time to pursue my dream of publication, but of late the desire and the compulsion to put words onto paper have once again dominated my life so that now, my laptop has become surgically fused to my fingertips.

There is something desperately satisfying about telling a story. My fascination with History, Religion and Conspiracy theories have, in this instance, gone hand-in-hand with my love of all things vampire, fantasy, sci-fi and horror. I drove my parents nuts when I was young because that was all I would read about in books, all I would watch on television, but they have held me in good stead, and long may my obsession with the subjects continue, at least, that is, until the day they put me in my own wooden box. And imagination is such a wonderful thing. I once had a rather vivid dream about David Tennant and the Tardis console, but I could not possibly go into details about that here. Let's just say that my polarity was well and truly reversed.

Dead Camp is just the beginning. I have to check my

knickers every day at the thought that this book is now in the public domain. My first book, and I hope the first of many. And to those out there who love to write, who love to transport us to new worlds, or old worlds with a twisted perspective, I say to you keep going. I never thought I would ever see my work available to download, and thanks to eXtasy Books, the dream that I always thought unobtainable has finally come true. So thank you all at eXtasy, I am one happy homosexual thanks to you, and thank you the reader for taking the time to read this strange tale and allowing Eli and the incomparable Malachi into your lives.

And now I really need Skyrim.